SO-AOC-994

The Boss on Redemption Road

Lane Walker

The Hometown Hunters Collection
www.lanewalkerbooks.com

The Boss on Redemption Road by Lane Walker
Copyright © 2014, 2021 Lane Walker

All rights reserved. This book is protected under the copyright laws of the United States of America. This book may not be copied or reprinted for commercial gain or profit.

ISBN 978-1-955657-03-7
For Worldwide Distribution
Printed in the U.S.A.

Published by Bakken Books
2021
www.lanewalkerbooks.com

To all kids and teens:
Unplug the electronics and plug into the great outdoors. Get out into the woods. A big world full of adventure is just waiting for you. You won't regret it! You were meant for so much more!

Special thanks to Owen S.
Your strength is inspirational, and your smile is contagious. I'm very blessed to know such an incredible young man.

For more books, check out:
www.lanewalkerbooks.com

-1-

Prologue

Enemy aliens have me surrounded!

I was backed in the corner of a dark room with no escape. They slowly crept closer and closer to me. I had to think fast because, if I didn't, my life was going to end.

Suddenly a loud noise erupted and caught my attention. I thought it was part of the massive alien attack, but it wasn't.

It was a knock on my bedroom door.

I paused my video game and went over to the door. I didn't like to be interrupted when I was playing video games, especially when I was playing a new one—*Earth vs. Aliens IV.*

"Who is it?" I yelled.

"It's Dad. We need to talk," he quickly replied.

That's strange. My parents don't usually bother me unless there's something important. *Am I in trouble? Did my school call? Why is Dad knocking on my bedroom door?*

Either way, I knew this visit wasn't going to be a good one. I could tell that Dad's tone was different. I slowly unlocked the door, and to my surprise, both of my parents were standing there.

"Have a seat, son; we have something we need to tell you," Dad said with a low sigh.

Why do they have to bug me when I'm playing video games? I'm a video game junkie. I'd play morning, noon, and night if my parents would let me.

I was just about to enter World Three in my new video game. I had pre-ordered the game and had spent the entire weekend trying to reach the third level. I was finally there, and now I had to pause it.

I went over to the video game console to shut off the game until I realized that Dad had already shut off the television. I turned to see what his problem was, but once I caught a glimpse of the look on his face, I stopped dead in my tracks.

Both Dad and Mom were now sitting on my bed.

"Hunter, come have a seat by us," my mom said sweetly.

I sat down. Now I was really starting to worry.

"Son, we have some bad news," my dad said. Talking was difficult for Dad; he wasn't crying, but he was as close to it as I had ever seen him.

"Okay, what's up?" I asked quickly.

My bed suddenly felt cold. A small chill crawled up my back and lodged in my throat.

"We found out today that the shop is closing. In two weeks, I won't have a job," Dad stated.

I could tell it was hard for him to tell his only son that he didn't have a job.

"Okay...well, thanks for letting me know," I replied.

As I started to get up, my mom reached out, grabbed my arm and motioned for me to sit back down.

———

"There's one more thing we need to tell you, Hunter," she said.

After an awkward silence, Dad looked at me and said something totally unexpected: "We're moving." The three of us sat motionless for a couple minutes, sharing an awkward silence until finally Dad cleared his throat and said again: "Hunter, we're moving."

-2-

Moving? How can this be? We've lived in down-town Denver my whole life.

"Moving? Like down the street or across town?" I quickly asked. I have never even traveled any-where—never left Denver. Ever!

"We're fortunate that our apartment lease is up at the end of this month, so we'll be free to move. We'll be going to a small town northwest of Denver called Pine Bluff. It's about twenty miles north of Craig," Dad explained.

Huh? Who or what is Craig? Sounds more like a person's name, not a city.

Northwest of Denver is nothing but open fields

and mountains. I learned in my social studies class in school that not much is found in that part of Colorado—just a bunch of small towns, cattle ranchers, and wild animals—none of which interested this city boy. I liked the bright lights, the busy streets, and I preferred to buy food from a grocery store or a local restaurant.

This all seems like a cruel joke, like I was on some really bad TV reality show.

"What's in Pine Bluff?" I asked.

"A free place to stay—somewhere we can go until we get back on our feet again. Your mom's Great-Uncle Otis has a small farmhouse there. Since he's living in a retirement home, the house is sitting empty. Grandma Elaine said Uncle Otis wouldn't mind and was nice enough to let us stay there until I can get back on my feet and find a job," Dad explained.

Nice enough? I guess that's a matter of opinion. I couldn't believe how fast my life was changing. I felt like I was stuck in the path of a raging tornado with no escape. I felt hopeless.

"So, I don't even have a choice in this move?" I asked.

"There aren't a lot of options, Hunter," Mom said.

They both got up and walked out of my room. Just as Dad was shutting the door, he took one last look in my direction. I could see the hurt on his face, but I was so mad I shot him one of the meanest looks I had ever given anyone. It made me feel good, but I saw the disappointment on his face. Dad dropped his head and shut the door behind him.

I laid down and stared at my ceiling, a million thoughts running through my mind.

-3-

I had a hard time getting to sleep that night after my parents broke the news about moving. The next morning, I woke up early for school even though I hated school, especially Mondays. I was hoping that the news from last night was nothing more than a bad dream.

I could smell fresh bacon sizzling on the stove in the kitchen. I knew instantly that it wasn't a dream; it was all too real. Mom only cooked breakfast on holidays and on days when something big happened. She greeted me when I walked into the kitchen. "Hey, honey, have a seat. I have your favorite breakfast—bacon and chocolate chip pancakes."

I let out a deep sigh.

"I was hoping it was all a nightmare, but I guess it wasn't," I said, rubbing my eyes.

Mom shook her head and told me, "You know, Hunter, this isn't easy on anyone, especially your dad. You might want to think about his feelings."

She was right. My dad was a hard worker and a great guy. A couple years ago we had started drifting apart. I used to be his little buddy. He's a football fanatic, and we always had spent our Sundays cheering on our favorite team—the Denver Broncos.

Up until then, I always had loved making snacks and wearing our blue and orange. But then something changed, and that something was me.

I stopped liking sports and started to spend a lot of time playing video games. Being an only child has some definite advantages, but when it came to finding someone or something to play with, I found video games were more fun.

I just didn't play video games—I was addicted. During the week I would think of ways to sneak in more time to play than I was allowed. On the weekends, however, when I had no restrictions, I played until the skin on my fingers was rubbed raw.

The rest of the month flew by. My parents spent their time selling most of our furniture and other belongings on eBay and packing up what little we were taking with us. Mom said Uncle Otis had left everything we would need. As for me, I spent my time in my room playing video games.

The last day before moving finally arrived. That morning, Mom was once again in the kitchen making breakfast. But this was no holiday; this was the last day of life as we all knew it. Who could tell what tomorrow would bring? Nothing good, I was sure of it.

"Honey," she said as she handed me the plate of food, "since this is your last day of school here in Denver, make sure you tell all your friends and Miss Brockway goodbye."

I didn't tell my mom but saying goodbye was going to be easy. I only need to tell three people—

probably the only three people on this earth who would even notice that I was gone. I figured it would take at least a week for Mr. Rawlings, the gym teacher, to realize that I wasn't sitting against the south wall.

The first one I wanted to tell was our janitor, Mr. Pete. He was one of the nicest people on this earth. He always greeted me and asked about my day. The second was Mrs. Holiday, one of the kitchen cooks. For some reason, she had always smiled warmly at me when I went through the lunch line.

The last one was Steve, who was probably the only friend I had. Steve and I had become buddies a couple of years ago and had a lot in common. The main love we shared was video games. He even stayed at my house once, and we played video games all night long. But even Steve and I weren't that close. The truth was, I didn't have many people I was close to.

The day went by fast. No one at school made a big deal about my moving; no one really seemed to care.

-4-

The long ride to Pine Bluff started out slow and seem to drag on. I felt like we were driving for months.

In all reality we had only driven a few hours, but it seemed like a long time. Maybe it was because it was the longest trip I had ever taken, or maybe it was because I hated the thought of leaving the city.

"Hunter, we're passing through Craig, so we aren't far now," Dad told me.

Craig was a small town by my terms, especially compared to Denver. The streets were lined with small restaurants and coffee shops.

As we drove through, I kept my eye open for

any video game or electronic stores. I didn't see even one and that discovery worried me.

The one thing I did like about Craig was all the elk stuff. It was everywhere, and, for some reason, I became fascinated with this animal called an elk. When Dad stopped to get gas, I went into the convenience store to use the bathroom. Throughout the store, I saw t-shirts, hats, and magazines plastered with pictures of elk.

I couldn't help but ask the gas station attendant, "Are there are a lot of elk around here?"

She looked up and giggled. "You must be new to these parts. There are elk everywhere. We have people that come from all over the country to hunt elk near Craig. See that gray van?" she asked, pointing outside.

I looked toward one of the gas pumps and nodded.

"Those folks have traveled twenty-eight hours— all the way from Michigan just to hunt elk in Craig," she said.

Cool. I skipped out to the car.

"What has gotten into you, Hunter?" Mom asked.

"Elk," I said. "And they're everywhere around here!"

Mom just looked surprised and smiled.

After fueling up, we traveled twenty miles deeper into the mountains. When Dad said we were about four or five miles from Pine Bluff, the road started to get a lot steeper. The incline was so sharp, it made me feel like I was being pushed back hard against my seat.

After a couple miles, the highway flattened out again, and I saw a small green sign that said, "Welcome to Pine Bluff—A Place That Everyone Calls Home."

Interesting.

I thought about it and even though I had lived in Denver for my entire life—all twelve years of it—it had never felt like home.

As we drove into Pine Bluff, I was surprised at how small it was. There were a couple stores, two gas stations, a pizza restaurant, and three churches. And that was about it. Mom and Dad could tell I was nervous.

"I'm sure there are lots of fun things to do here, honey," Mom quickly said.

I wasn't nervous—I was terrified! I could already tell there was nothing to do in this little town with only two traffic lights, and one of them didn't even work!

"Our place is three miles out of town on a road called Redemption Road," Dad said.

"Since we don't have any groceries, let's stop in and have some pizza before heading to the house," Mom suggested.

That proposal sounded like a great idea. I was starving and loved pizza.

"Well, what will it be tonight?" asked Dad. "Our choices are Paul's Pizzeria or Paul's Pizzeria." He smiled for the first time on the trip.

Although I had been stoked at all the elk stuff I had seen, now I had a sinking feeling it wouldn't take long to get sick of pizza and tired of Pine Bluff.

We pulled into the tiny pizzeria and noticed

several other cars in the parking lot. I guess when you're the only pizza joint in town, you get busy.

When we walked in, everyone stopped talking and eating and stared at us. It was weirdly quiet and obvious that they all knew we were outsiders. I figured that not many new people visited Paul's Pizzeria. We found a booth near the back of the restaurant. Old country music played over the speakers, and I felt like we were in downtown Hicksville. I was worried what wild animals they used as meat on the pizza.

"Hi ya, folks! Welcome to Paul's. My name is Trinity, and I'll be your waitress tonight. Are you new here or just passing through?" she asked.

"We plan to stay here for a while and hopefully call Pine Bluff home. We're moving to the Smith Farm on Redemption Road," Dad said.

I rolled my eyes. *This hick town will never be my home,* I thought.

The waitress stopped instantly and turned to my dad with a shocked look on her face. "Where did you say you're moving to?" she quickly asked.

"Redemption Road," Dad said, puzzled at her awkward response.

"Oh, I see. Okay, I'll be back in a minute to take your order," the suddenly frazzled waitress said.

In an instant, she went from being cute and bubbly to just plain weird. Something bothered her about what Dad had said about Redemption Road. Mom and Dad had noticed it too. They shared glances with each other.

Finally, I spoke up. "Boy, that was strange. She acted like she had seen a ghost or something," I said.

Whatever the reason, I had a feeling that our adventure was about to take a turn for the worse.

I wasn't sure I wanted to know what mystery and danger lived on Redemption Road, but like it or not, we were about to find out.

-5-

"Did you say *Redemption Road?*" a stranger who was sitting at a nearby table asked.

"Yes," my dad answered, puzzled.

The man looked around and slowly got up. He came over and sat in the chair next to me. "Have you folks ever been down Redemption Road?" the man asked.

"No, we're from Denver. Otis Smith is my wife's uncle, and we're staying in his farmhouse," Dad responded.

The man nodded. "I figured," he said.

"Figured what?" Dad quickly asked.

"There are only two houses on Redemption

Road. The old Smith place and the other one…" The man's voice trailed off. We stared at the stranger, waiting for some sort of explanation.

He offered none, so I asked, "What's the deal with Redemption Road?"

The man took a deep breath and sat back in the chair. He yelled for Trinity to bring him another coffee, straight black. He cracked his neck slowly and leaned forward.

"*She* lives on Redemption Road," answered the stranger.

She who? This whole conversation was odd. There was something strange too about the people of Pine Bluff. In the city, people are much more direct.

"*Crazy Kate!* That's who lives out on Redemption Road. She's the nastiest, meanest lady in the world. You don't want anything to do with her, trust me. She'll eat you for dinner, boy," the man said.

Gulp! That's the last thing I wanted to hear. Not only were we moving out to the middle of nowhere

where people act strange, now I find out our only neighbor is a woman named Crazy Kate.

This bad dream had officially turned into a full-blown nightmare. I glanced at my dad out of the corner of my eye. I was waiting to see what his response would be.

"Well, thanks for the heads up, friend," he said quietly, "but we'll form our own opinion about our neighbors and other people in this town."

With that comment, the mysterious man stood and walked out of the restaurant.

What a first day in Pine Bluff!

I barely ate any of my pizza—even though it was really good. It was much different than the restaurant chain pizza in Denver, and I really liked it. But it was hard to eat as my thoughts kept circling back to how the stranger had called our neighbor "Crazy Kate."

You have to earn a nickname like that; it can't come very easily. When I was in second grade, a kid named Steve got the nickname Stinky. Trust me, he deserved every ounce of that nickname. Stinky would go out of his way to let everyone know what he had for breakfast, lunch, and dinner. But Crazy Kate was a nickname that sent shivers down by spine.

The waitress brought us several boxes to take the rest of the pizza home. She must have figured that we didn't have any groceries or food at the house.

"Thanks, but I think you're forgetting something," Dad said.

"Oh, honey, there's no charge on your pizza tonight. You folks are gonna need all the help you can get. Welcome to Pine Bluff!" said the waitress.

-6-

When we got into the car, everyone was quiet. It was dark so I couldn't look for any wild animals or admire the nearby mountains. We headed south out of town toward Redemption Road. After about three miles, we saw an old beat-up sign nailed to a telephone pole. The words were faded, but I could just make out the letters *p-t-i-o-n* and knew this had to be it.

As we turned onto the road, it was obvious not much traffic was using it. Uncle Otis had been living in a Florida nursing home for the past year, so we already knew the house would probably need some serious work to bring it back to life.

We drove down the isolated dirt road that seemed to get darker and darker. The shadows of the nearby mountains cast a black cloud over the entire road. The road was long and winding, and there was no sign of life. After a couple of miles, I could barely make out a small glow in the distance.

As we approached the glow, I could tell it was an old porch light. The house was set off the road, with a broken-down picket fence surrounding it. Dad stopped in front of the house, trying to make out the address on the mailbox.

I thought for sure this must be Uncle Otis' house. Junk was everywhere. It looked like someone hadn't lived there in a while. The windows had cracks, and the front porch was lopsided.

Dad turned the car so the headlights would illuminate the mailbox. There written in bold red letters was the name MAXWELL.

"Nope, this isn't our place," Dad said as he put the car back in drive and headed down the road.

If it isn't our place, then it has to be Crazy Kate's!

The man at the restaurant had said only two people lived on that road.

Dad pulled slowly away, looking in the distance for any other lights or mailboxes.

I watched out the back window as we left the Maxwell house. Something was weird about it. Even if the stranger hadn't warned us, I would have sensed something evil about the place. Something just wasn't quite right there.

We drove on another mile or so until we came to another old mailbox. It was so dark there I couldn't even see where the house was. This time the name on the mailbox read SMITH, and we knew we were in the right place. Dad slowly turned into the driveway, and the headlights suddenly lighted up a house.

The house looked old and rough but not falling down—not yet at least. It wasn't as bad as I thought it would look. The house was light blue and had white shutters. It actually looked pretty well kept from the outside compared to the other house we had just seen.

"Well, at least there are no major surprises with the house," Mom said.

Dad went inside to turn on the lights but returned after a few minutes.

"It looks like the electricity isn't on. With all the stuff we had to do to get ready to move, I forgot to call the electric company here. I'll have to go over there in the morning and have them turn the power back on," Dad explained.

No electricity! One spooky house in the middle of nowhere plus a crazy neighbor—all these things sounded like the beginnings of a perfect horror movie.

"We're going to have to sleep in the car tonight," Dad said.

What? No way was I sleeping in the car.

"No, that isn't going to happen," I quickly said.

"Well, Hunter, we have two options: either we can sleep in the car, or we can go to our new neighbor and see if she has any flashlights we could borrow for the night."

"The car will be fine!" I decided quickly.

When he put it that way, I had no choice. There was no way I wanted to go to a stranger's house this late at night—especially a house owned by someone named Crazy Kate.

I climbed into the back seat and grabbed a blanket from the back. The temperature was cool but not cold. Dad and Mom reclined their seats back and tried to settle in.

I had trouble falling asleep, and it wasn't because we were sleeping in our car. Every time I closed my eyes, I pictured a crazy, gray-haired lady peeking into the car.

Just as I started to drift off to sleep, I heard a terrifying noise. Something was howling and screaming close by.

"What was that?" I asked.

"It's just some coyotes; go to sleep," Dad said.

Just some coyotes? Great, now we're surrounded by savage wild animals!

-7-

I tossed and turned all night, worrying about the nearby coyotes. Morning finally came, and I awakened to a different sound. But this one didn't scare me—it was majestic! I just knew it was the call of a large elk! I later learned that hunters called it an *elk bugle*). Even though we never saw the elk that day, I knew two things: he must have been really big, and he was very close to our house.

After we made a quick trip into town the next morning to get the electricity turned on and buy a few more items, we were once again back at our new home.

"I guess we should start unpacking the car. Well,

let's go see what our new house looks like," Dad suggested.

We started unloading all of our possessions—at least the few we still had. I was extra careful carrying one box because it held all my video game stuff. That box was the only thing I cared about. I couldn't let anything happen to those games. I didn't want to be stuck in the middle of nowhere without them. They were my only saving grace—the one thing that would probably keep me from going nuts.

I was surprised as I went inside the old farmhouse. It wasn't quite as bad as I had imagined. There had even been some modest updates in the kitchen, but the carpet was really old.

"Don't worry, Son, these colors will once again come back in style," Dad said with a smile.

I laughed. There was no way anyone would ever pay money to put this stuff in their house!

The house was simple. It had two bedrooms and one small bathroom. The best part was the large family room. The ceilings were higher than the other rooms, and the entire back wall had been designed with windows that faced the mountains. It seemed like whoever had built the house had known how amazing the view would be.

Mom and Dad started unpacking the food we had bought, and I went to my room to set up my video games. I was still trying to beat two of my games. I mostly liked role-playing games because they made me feel like I was important—like I was someone who mattered.

When I power on my games, all my fears go away, and I turn into a different person. I loved how even while sitting in a small apartment in downtown Denver, I could experience an adventure anywhere in the world. If only my video games were actually real!

To be honest, I wasn't brave or outgoing. At my former school, I was basically a nobody. I had one friend, and few things excited me.

But the one consistent thing in my life was my video games. I was the best; I was the hero who was going to save the princess.

"Come on, Hunter, really?" Dad said angrily as he came into my room with a box.

"What?" I sarcastically answered.

"You know what. Shut those stupid video games off! We just got here."

Stupid video games? The one thing that I loved, the one thing I was actually good at, and my dad hated them. I think he was jealous that I would rather be playing video games than spending time with him watching his stupid football games.

Mom happened to be going down the hall and turned in to my room to see what was going on.

"Leave him alone, honey; let him get adjusted," my mom said.

My mom almost always sided with me, and I was glad she came and bailed me out. I could tell our conversation was going to get heated up otherwise, and we'd end up in an argument.

Dad just shook his head and walked out. I spent the rest of the afternoon trying to beat my video game Warriors Challenge 13. I got close a couple of times but couldn't do it. After several hours of playing, my eyes started hurting. I paused the game to go get something to eat.

As I went out to the kitchen to look for a snack, I could hear talking outside. I couldn't see who it was, so I quietly went to the front door. I slowly turned the handle and stepped out onto the porch. I went down the steps trying not to be seen, but the old boards made a loud creaking sound. The talking abruptly stopped, and two people came around the corner of the house.

The woman looked unkempt. She had a huge mole beneath her nose, and though I tried with all my might, it was hard not to stare at it.

"Son, come over here. I have someone I want you to meet," Dad said.

I slowly walked over and extended my hand.

The woman just scowled.

"Nice to meet you. My name is Hunter," I quickly said.

"Katherine, but most people call me Kate. Well, actually they call me a lot of things around this crummy little town," the lady said.

Great. It was Crazy Kate, and she was living up to everything the townspeople had told us.

In fact, she was even worse in person. She was rougher than anyone I had ever met. I tried not to make eye contact with her. As soon as she'd told me her name, my mouth dropped, and she saw it.

It was like she knew people had already warned us about her. I stood there quietly for what seemed like forever. It was awkward, and I wanted to get out of the situation. I didn't want to be around our new neighbor.

She didn't exactly glow with friendliness. Most new neighbors would bring you a pie or cookies or something sweet to welcome them.

"I'm going to head back inside," I finally said.

Dad nodded and Kate turned her head.

"What do you have to do that's so important?" Kate muttered.

"I'm just taking a break from Warriors Challenge 13. I almost beat Zooron, the boss of World Four. If I can beat him, I'll get the key to Calcutta," I said with a smile.

Kate gave me a dirty look. I knew I had made a huge mistake as soon as I said it. Kate had no idea what Warriors Challenge 13 was. I bet she'd never even played a video game in her entire life.

"What kind of kid are you raising?" she asked Dad. "Go back in the house, you big geek," she yelled at me.

I was startled. I slowly backed up, using my foot to feel for the porch steps. I was shaking hard and so scared, I clumsily tripped over the first step that was sticking out.

I scrambled to my feet, turned, and raced back up the steps. All I could hear was Crazy Kate's evil laugh.

"Maybe you should spend less time on the TV and more time outside!" she shouted.

I ran back inside to my bedroom and the comfort of my video games.

-8-

Once again, just when I thought things couldn't get worse for me in this hillbilly town, they did. My video game froze. I must have had it paused too long, so now I had to start back at the beginning of level four! Hours and hours of playing, and now I was back where I had started.

That was it. *I've had enough!* I was tired of this stupid town, hated my grouchy, nasty neighbor, and had about all I could deal with.

Without thinking I reached back and slammed my video game controller to the floor. To my horror, it shattered into a million pieces and scattered across the room.

The noise was louder than I thought, and my dad came running in.

"What happened?" he asked.

He could tell I was steaming mad.

"I'm sick of this place already! This is your fault. Why did you have to ruin everything and make us leave Denver?" I yelled.

Dad was shocked that I had raised my voice to him. I could tell he didn't know what to say, so he just stood quietly for a few seconds.

He finally broke the awkward silence. "I guess this means that I don't have to worry about you spending all day and night playing your video games," he said in a low voice.

I was shocked. He didn't seem angry at me or have any guilt for bringing us to this crummy old house.

"What do you mean? You just need to buy me a new controller," I quickly said.

"Not any time soon, Hunter. We don't have the money for any video game controllers," he said.

I couldn't believe what he said.

We don't have money to buy one video game controller? "Are you kidding me? How long are you going to make me wait?" I asked.

Mom walked in and looked at me.

"Mom?" I pleaded.

She looked at me and then took one look at the floor and the scattered bits of plastic.

"I'm leaving this one up to your dad. When he says you can get a new one, you can," she said and left Dad and me in the room alone.

I knew I was in big trouble now. Mom had almost always bailed me out before, but there was no getting around this situation.

"You can get a new controller as soon as *you* earn the money for it," Dad stated.

Earn the money? How in the world was I going to earn the money in this town? There were like two stores and who would hire a 12-year-old city kid anyway?

I ran through the house and out the front, slamming the door behind me. I didn't know where I was going, but I knew I wasn't going to stay inside.

But where can I go? I had no idea what was around us besides thick forests and high mountains.

When I looked around, an old barn on the back edge of our property caught my eye. It was weathered and beat up, like most of the buildings in Pine Bluff, but at least it gave me a place to go and hide for now.

The big door was hard to move, but after a lot of pushing and pulling, it slowly swung open. I was surprised at how clean the inside was. It seemed to be like a lot of the buildings around here—rough on the outside but nice on the inside.

Just seeing the outside, you would think that the old barn should be torn down and burned, but that wasn't the case. The inside was in great shape and had a bunch of old stuff in it. Some farm equipment was neatly parked along one wall. The barn itself had huge beams and a high loft at the top. I wondered what stories the old barn would tell if it could talk.

I decided to explore every nook and cranny and discovered some cool stuff. When I reached the back of the barn, I noticed a small door that was undersized. It looked like it was just made for a 12-year-old kid.

The dusty doorknob was rough and hard to turn. After trying with all my might, I got the knob to turn finally, and the door creaked open.

The open door let the sunlight from the barn into the room, and it made me wonder how long it had been since the hidden room had seen daylight. The sunlight cast a yellow glow on the room, and I was amazed to see a huge pile of antlers stacked in the middle of the floor.

I walked over and picked up one of the bigger sets. I had never held antlers before and was surprised at how heavy they were to hold.

I trembled with excitement as I held them up to examine them. They were fascinating. They had six protrusions on one side and seven on the other. (I found out later that the protrusions were called *points*.)

Although this was the biggest pair, there had to be at least twenty more sets; some were much smaller and looked different. I guessed they were deer antlers, and the bigger ones were elk.

Whoever got these big bucks must have been a great hunter. I wondered if it was Uncle Otis. I couldn't help but think about the wonderful stories that these horns could tell. I went through the entire pile and held every pair. I laid them out and started putting them in rows to organize them.

That's when I noticed something in the corner. It looked like an old army tarp that was a faded olive-green. The tarp was so well camouflaged, I hadn't noticed it at first.

I couldn't resist. I walked over to the tarp and ripped off the cover. I couldn't believe what I saw!

-9-

I stood staring. Hidden underneath the old tarp was a large cedar chest. It wasn't anything fancy, but the chest looked old, weathered, and mysterious. There were no carvings or any type of identifiers—just one rusty-looking hinge where a lock had once been.

As I opened the lid, the chest made a low, moaning sound. Whoever had owned the chest had taken great care of their belongings. Everything was neatly packed and arranged inside.

I reached down and the first item I pulled out was some type of clothing. It looked like an old button-up shirt—something a cowboy would wear. There were a couple of shirts and a pair of overalls, nothing too interesting, so I put them to the side.

I reached farther into the chest, and my hand hit something hard that made a solemn echo every time I touched it. I realized it was a small cardboard box—probably about the size of a boot box. I grabbed the box, expecting to feel the weight of boots but didn't. I shook it, and there was something in it, but it wasn't boots. Whatever was inside was much lighter.

I slowly opened the box, and to my surprise it was a hat—not just any hat, an actual Stetson cowboy hat! The hat was brown, and even though it looked really old, it still held its shape perfectly. I had seen a lot of cowboy hats. My dad is obsessed with old cowboy movies and watches them all the time he's not watching sports. I think the movies are boring. The only part I like is when the cowboy captures all the outlaws and becomes a hero.

I set the hat down and continued digging through the chest. There were more clothes and a bunch of old newspapers. I wondered why someone had kept the papers. I thought maybe something was important in them. I figured if they were junk, someone would have used them to start a fire. I threw everything back into the chest, except the hat and the box of newspapers. I slowly made my way back to the house with the box.

Dad was sitting in a chair, watching an old western and thumbing through the local newspaper, *The Pine Bluff Press*. I stopped and looked into my box. The newspapers I had found were old copies of the exact same newspaper. The logo had changed, the layout looked totally different, but it was the same newspaper for sure.

"Dad, look what I found!" I said excitedly.

He could tell that I was really excited, and it seemed like he wanted to forget about our earlier blowup. "Cool, Hunter, that hat is so you!" Dad said with a smile.

I set the hat down and walked over and started laying out the newspapers.

"Wow! There are some really old ones! This one

is from 1958. Look at these ads! I sure wish bread was still nineteen cents and a gallon of gas was twenty-four cents," Dad said.

Mom put down her dishtowel and came over. We started thumbing through the papers together. There were all kinds of neat articles about Pine Bluff.

"Would you look at that—there's Uncle Otis," Mom said as she pointed toward the front page of one of the older newspapers. The paper was really frail and was starting to come apart and break into a bunch of little flakes.

There were too many newspapers to go through quickly, so I grabbed the rest of them and placed everything back into the old cardboard box. I went to my room and eventually stashed the box under my bed. Before I started to get ready for bed, I turned on my video game. I figured that I just had time to play a couple games of Warriors Challenge 13. Then I remembered about the broken controller.

Turning off the TV and feeling depressed, I went and got the old cowboy hat and slipped it on.

I went over and looked in the mirror. I felt different. My chest stuck out a little farther, and I stood straighter. For a split second, I actually looked and felt like someone ready to tame the Wild West, a hero out of one of my dad's old western movies.

"Hunter, that looks really good on you," Mom said.

I turned to see her standing in the doorway. I quickly took the hat off and threw it on the bed.

"It's time for bed. Tomorrow's going to be a busy day," said Mom.

I had forgotten all about tomorrow. School was tomorrow.

I was going to be the new kid, and I knew it was going to be hard for a new kid to hide in a small town like this.

-10-

The next morning, I was up before my alarm clock went off, feeling nervous about starting at a new school. I didn't want to be the new kid. Those kids were fresh meat, and everyone wanted to see what they were about. That didn't interest me. I had always been a loner and wanted to keep it that way.

Dad was up early, making breakfast. I sat down at the table. I was thinking about telling him I was sick or something, but I knew he would see right through that.

"Dad, how am I going to make money to buy a new controller? They cost like fifty dollars!"

I could tell by the look on my dad's face he had

no clue they cost that much. I guess Mom had probably bought a lot of my gaming stuff without telling Dad how expensive it was.

"You might have to do what I'm doing and try to find a job. We don't have the money to buy one now, Hunter. I'm just trying to keep food on the table," Dad said with a frown.

I nodded. I kind of felt bad, but in the back of my mind I still wanted to get a new controller.

"Finish eating, son, and get your shoes on. The bus will be here any minute."

Bus? I've never ridden a school bus before. In Denver there were very few school buses; most of us walked to school. I wondered why my dad hadn't told me about it before. I scrambled to my feet and shoved the toast in my mouth. I ran toward the front door just in time to see a flashing light coming down the road. The bus came to a screeching halt, and I heard a loud horn blare.

I couldn't tie my shoes fast enough as I stumbled out the front door. Just as I was about to clear the last step, I tripped and went tumbling to the ground. I jumped up, hoping no one on the bus had seen me.

I jogged down the driveway toward the bus. The door slowly opened, and I was greeted by the bus driver. He was an older man and smelled like a mixture of oil and old bread.

"Morning, son, I'm Mr. Jenkins. We're already running late. Make sure you're standing out at your mailbox on time tomorrow," the man said.

I nodded and started down the aisle. A lot of kids were already on the bus. I walked slowly, hoping someone would offer their seat, but no one did.

"Sit down, boy; I don't want you to fall again," Mr. Jenkins yelled.

The entire busload of kids started laughing. I rushed to the first seat that was open and sat down. I leaned against the window and watched as the countryside passed by quickly while Mr. Jenkins drove toward the school.

I couldn't believe how bad my first day had started out. About five minutes later, I felt the bus slam to a complete stop.

I heard the front door open, and I continued to stare out the window when I felt a tap on my shoulder. I turned to see this giant kid glaring at me. He had to be six feet, three inches, and looked bigger than most seniors. Not only was he big, but he already had a full mustache.

"Hey, City Boy, you're sitting in my seat!"

How does this kid know I'm from the city? I didn't know what to do, but I had to do something. Either I was going to be a coward, or I was going to stand up to this big kid and let everyone know that no one messes with this city boy. It took me a second, but I said the first thing that came in my mind.

"Oh, yeah? I don't see your name on it!"

The whole bus echoed with the loud gasping sound of multiple voices, and I knew I was in big trouble. The kid looked around, surprised that some new kid had mouthed back to him. Without warning, I felt his huge cold hands grab the back of my neck and shove my face into the bus seat in front of me. He was strong, and I couldn't move.

"What's that say, City Boy?"

I squinted as I tried to make out the words scribbled on the seat. I could barely make it out, but I could slowly start to make out some letters: *M-A-X*. I guess his name was on the seat.

-11-

The bus driver yelled something toward us, giving me enough time to break free. I quickly jumped up and went over to a seat with two little kids. I guessed they were probably kindergartners. They started laughing and so did the rest of the bus riders. I sat down and didn't look back the entire ride to school. As soon as we parked, I bolted from my seat to get off the bus. I wanted to get as far away from Max as possible.

"Don't worry, kid; Max isn't so bad," Mr. Jenkins said with a grin. I nodded and stepped off the bus. The school had a brick front and was much older than the school I had attended in Denver. My school in Denver was only two years old and had all the newest technology features. I was hoping Pine Bluff at least had indoor plumbing.

I walked in the front door and into the main office. A rosy-cheeked, older lady was sitting behind the front desk. She wore bright clothes and had on an old-style broach.

"May I help you?" she smiled and asked. I must have stood out pretty bad. School had already been in session for a month, and I don't think they have too many new kids move to Pine Bluff.

"Yes, my name is Hunter. I'm new and don't know where I'm supposed to go."

The lady walked over to a nearby file cabinet and grabbed a manila folder.

"Yes, here it is. I see you're in sixth grade," she said.

I nodded. It was obvious they'd already gotten my records from my school in Denver.

As she looked through my folder, her original friendly manner started to change. "*This* says your address is 3645 Redemption Road. Is that correct?"

she asked. Her voice quickly changed from friendly and confident to quivery and nervous. "Is that correct?" she asked again.

"Yes, I live on Redemption Road," I said.

She rolled her chair over to a nearby phone. I couldn't hear what she was saying, but seconds later I saw a door open behind her and out walked a man with a shirt and tie.

"Hello, my name is Mr. Wilson. I'm the principal at Pine Bluff. Did I hear you're living on Redemption Road?" he asked.

"Yes, sir, we live on my Uncle Otis' old farm."

"That's interesting. I knew you were moving in from the city, but I guess I never checked your new address. Have you met your neighbor yet?" he quickly asked.

I knew what the problem was. "Oh, yeah, I met Kate. She's really charming," I said with a smile.

Mr. Wilson laughed and put his hand on my back. "I feel sorry for you. Crazy Kate is the craziest lady I have ever met; steer clear of her."

He didn't need to tell me that. I had already

planned on staying as far away from Crazy Kate as possible.

He added, "If you have any questions about our school, let me know."

This was my chance. I was going to get this bully in trouble and that would stop him from picking on me.

"Mr. Wilson, I had this problem with a boy on the bus. I think his name was Max," I said.

Mr. Wilson stopped and looked at me. "What kind of problem did you have?" he asked.

I explained the whole story. I was hoping he'd pull Max in and tell him if he ever touched me again, he'd expel him from school.

But that didn't happen.

"I'll have a talk with him," Mr. Wilson said with an air of finality.

"Is there any way you could talk to him before the bus ride home?"

"No, I don't think so. I will have a talk with him tonight, though, when we get home from school," he explained.

"When you get home?"

"Max is my son. Welcome to Pine Bluff Schools, *City Boy!*" he said with a sarcastic grin.

-12-

Walking into my new classroom for the first time was horrible. The door creaked loudly, and everyone stopped what they were doing to stare at me. I was the center of attention, and I didn't like it. There were only about fifteen kids in the class, which seemed small. Back in Denver, I had like forty kids in my class.

My teacher introduced himself as Mr. Peavey and welcomed me with a smile, motioning me to an empty desk near the back of the room.

I was happy to have a desk waiting for me; it made me feel like they were expecting me. Mr. Peavey started back into his math lesson, and I tried to follow along. I could slowly feel the eyes shifting off me and back to the front of the room.

The morning went by pretty fast, and before I knew it, Mr. Peavey announced, "It's 11:00 a.m. boys and girls; it's time for recess."

A small cheer went out through the class. Most sixth graders love recess, and I usually did too but not this time. I was afraid of recess—well, not so much recess as Max.

Everyone rushed out of the room toward the playground. I slowly wandered to the hallway with my book bag and peeked around the corner toward the office and main hall.

Three boys from my class were waiting for me. They were all much bigger than I was, and they looked rough. I watched them whispering together; they looked like they were hatching some devious plan.

Not again, I thought. I knew they were talking about me. *Why is everyone here so mean?* First Max, and now this rough group of sixth graders. I couldn't catch a break. Suddenly one of them saw me peeking around the corner. He motioned to the others, and they started walking my way.

I scanned the hallways for the nearest escape route. I turned to go back into Mr. Peavey's room. I knew I could find safety there. The light was off, and, as I started to wiggle the doorknob, I could tell it was locked. I was too late—Mr. Peavey must have already left for his lunch.

When I turned back around, I knew I didn't have much time. They were closing in on me. I noticed one of the boys split from the group and start to circle around me. I could tell he was trying to cut me off from escaping. Then the larger boy started my way. He was wearing ripped jeans and a camouflage t-shirt.

My mind was racing with all the horrible things they were probably going to do to me—the new city kid.

"Hey!" the boy yelled as he inched closer and closer. His voice was deep and startled me.

I'm in big trouble. I had been backed in a corner without a lot of options. I didn't have time to think.

I took my book bag and threw it at the large boy who was coming toward me and took off running for the office. I put a spin move on the boy who had circled and never looked back. I could hear the boys yelling things, but I didn't know what they were saying, nor did I care. I was safe again. I ran in the office and sat down.

"May I help you?" asked the same secretary that I had met earlier in the morning.

"I was wondering if I could use the phone to call home," I said. I was thinking that I could talk my mom into coming and saving me from Pine Bluff School.

But before she handed me the phone, I remembered we didn't have a phone hooked up yet and cell service didn't work in the valley where we lived. There was no way of talking to my parents, no rescue in sight. *It's up to me to survive this place.*

I handed her back the phone and walked out. *But where am I going to go?* The hallways were empty, and I didn't even know where the cafeteria was.

I had a brainstorm! I knew where I could go. I snuck down to the boys' bathroom in our hallway, all the while keeping my eyes peeled for the three guys who had tried to jump me. The bathroom was directly across from our classroom. I walked to the back of the stall and quickly locked it. I put the toilet seat down and sat down. I pulled my feet up so no one would see me.

This was something I had done a lot in Denver. I often hid out in the bathroom to avoid people. After about ten minutes, I heard another bell ring and the hallway filled with commotion. Kids started coming in from outside, and I knew it was lunchtime. I thought I could jump in with the crowd and follow them to the cafeteria. I put my feet down and went to unlock the stall.

Just as I was pulling the lock back, I heard voices and footsteps coming into the bathroom. I quickly relocked the door and sat back down on the toilet seat.

I could barely make out what they were saying so I ducked down on the floor. I could see three different pairs of shoes. It was the boys who had tried getting me during recess!

"What's going on with that new kid?" one of the boys asked.

"I have no idea; I heard he is a city boy. Maybe they act like that in the city," another boy said.

"What are we going to do now, Owen?" someone asked.

There was a short pause, and I heard the familiar deep voice of the large boy.

"Maybe he doesn't know we're the official welcoming committee for Pine Bluff Elementary School. We need to give him a proper welcome."

-13-

I sat in that bathroom stall alone through the entire lunch period. My lunch was in my locker, and I wasn't going to risk my life to get it. *I hate this place!*

"Just give it a chance, honey, I'm sure there are all kinds of great kids at your new school," Mom had told me.

Yeah, right! If trying to kill me makes them great kids, then this school is overflowing with love.

I was fighting back the tears. There was no way I would cry on my first day of school like I was some baby in kindergarten or something. If I did, I'd never be able to live that down, and it would give all these bullies even more things to tease me about.

I don't know how long I sat there, but it seemed like a long time. Finally, I heard shuffling and noise coming down the hallway. I could tell kids were starting to return to Mr. Peavey's room.

This is my opportunity. The bathroom was empty, so I slowly unlocked the door and headed for the exit.

When I entered the classroom, I noticed the three boys who tried to get me before lunch talking to Mr. Peavey. I could tell they were talking about me because every once in a while, one would look at me. The largest one did most of the talking. The other two were smaller—even smaller than I was. I had seen this too many times in school at Denver. It was usually the biggest kid and his little cronies who would torment kids like me.

Why are they talking to the teacher? Are they telling on me for throwing my book bag or running down the hall?

I just wanted to be left alone! I had already come

to grips with the fact that I wasn't going to fit in or have any friends.

I couldn't hide in Pine Bluff; there was nowhere to go. But I wasn't going to be tortured for the rest of the school year by all these country kids. Maybe I could beg my mom to homeschool me.

"Hunter, can I see you in the hallway?" Mr. Peavey asked.

The whole class went quiet and stared at me as I walked out the door.

First, I was getting harassed by all these mean kids, and now I was going to get in trouble for trying to save myself.

"Hunter, how's it going? I know how hard it is to be the new kid," Mr. Peavey said.

How would he know? He's a teacher; he wouldn't know anything about being the new kid.

"When I was growing up, my dad was in the Air Force, so we moved all the time. By the time I graduated high school, I had been in more than eight schools," said Mr. Peavey.

Okay, maybe he does know, I thought.

"It's been a tough day," I admitted, fighting back the tears.

"I'm sure it has. Do me a favor, Hunter. Don't assume anything about Pine Bluff. I think if you really give it a chance, you'll like it," said Mr. Peavey.

He motioned into the classroom. I peeked around him to see the three boys coming toward me. I looked up at Mr. Peavey who smiled back. His smile was comforting, and I knew I was safe.

The three boys walked up and stood next to us.

"I'm going to leave you boys alone so you can talk," he said as he walked back into the room.

How could a teacher leave me alone with these kids?

-14-

The largest of the three walked up to me and extended his hand. "Hi, my name is Owen, and these are my friends, Jesse and Tom. We're sorry we scared you earlier. We were just going to see if you wanted to play basketball with us during recess," explained Owen.

What? The entire time I had thought these boys were after me. Even though Owen had a deep voice, it was honest and sincere. He was tall and strong. I could tell he was one of the biggest kids in the sixth grade.

"Are you serious?" I quickly asked.

"Yeah, I promise, we wouldn't hurt a flea. Well,

unless you're Max Wilson. I wouldn't mind hurting him," Owen mumbled.

We all laughed. It made me feel good to know that I wasn't the only one who had problems with Max. I looked at one of the smaller boys—the one who had tried to grab me.

"But you guys were circling me, and you tried to get me," I said motioning to the boy.

"Sorry about that. I was actually trying to go around you to go the bathroom. I couldn't hold it anymore," confessed Jesse.

"Anyway, we wanted to welcome you and let you know you're going to like it here. You can hang out with us, and we'll show you around," said Owen.

I couldn't help but smile. I couldn't believe how everything had changed for the better so quickly. I had totally judged these kids all wrong; they were cool!

"Where do you live?" Tom asked.

"I live at the end of Redemption Road on my great-uncle's farm."

All three boys froze. For a second, I thought

Max was sneaking up behind me. But I quickly remembered that everyone had the same expression when they found out where I lived.

Owen spoke up, "That's where Boss lives."

"I know, I know. I've already met her. Crazy Kate is my neighbor." I wanted to say it before the boys had a chance.

The boys looked at each other and nodded.

Finally, Owen spoke up. "You're right about old Kate. But she isn't Boss," he said.

He quickly added, "Boss is a legendary elk around this part of the state. He's the biggest, baddest bull elk in Colorado. No one can get close to him because no one is stupid enough to trespass on Crazy Kate's property."

Tom piped up, "No elk is worth your life!"

Thinking about this conversation later, I wondered if I would ever encounter Boss. For some reason, I was drawn to the woods and the mountains that surrounded Pine Bluff. The idea of hunting and being in the outdoors really fascinated me. It was something I wanted to try. I didn't know how or where to start, but every time someone started talking about the elk or the mountains, I could almost hear the bugle of the bull elk.

It seemed like his bugle was calling me, begging me to follow him into the wilderness.

-15-

I glanced up at the clock and saw that it read 2:55 p.m., which meant I only had five minutes before the end of the school day and before I saw Max again.

My first day at Pine Bluff had been memorable. The day had started off badly but turned out a lot better than I had thought it was going to be. Owen, Tommy, and Jesse seemed like kids who could be my friends—real friends. I already had more friends than I did in Denver!

Ring! Ring! Ring! The annoying sound of the school bell spooked me. It reminded me of the alarm clock on my wristwatch. I hated the annoying noise, but it always served its purpose. Now this alarm served a much different purpose.

"Have a great day. Remember to do page 43 in your math workbooks. I'll see you tomorrow," said Mr. Peavey.

Will he see me tomorrow? Max was really mad and told me he was going to get me back on the bus ride home today. This kid looked crazy—like someone who would hang the new kid out the window of a moving bus. It was even worse now because I knew that his daddy would protect him, and he wouldn't get in trouble. It was a bad combination—an oversized bully whose dad was the principal. It didn't look good for me.

I slowly walked toward my locker, grabbed my jacket, and scanned the hallway for any sign of Max. I didn't see him.

Maybe he got in trouble or isn't riding the bus home today, I quickly thought to myself. I was almost in the clear. Just before I stepped out the front door, I felt a hand grab my shoulder.

I turned to see Mr. Wilson.

"How was your first day, son?" he asked.

Do you mean besides your son almost killing me on the bus?

"Good, sir," I quickly replied.

I didn't need to make any more enemies at Pine Bluff for sure. He could tell I was nervous around him, and there was more that I wasn't telling him.

"Don't worry about Max. He just likes to have fun," he said with a grin.

I nodded and ran to my bus. We all sat and waited for the school to empty, but to my surprise there was no sign of the bully.

Suddenly the bus radio blared out, "All Pine Bluff buses, please continue to wait. One student still needs to get on the bus," announced Principal Wilson. My stomach sank, and it felt like I was going to throw up.

Without warning, the big main doors of the school flung open and out strutted Max. There was something about him, something that struck fear into everyone on the bus. The entire bus went quiet as Max slowly boarded the bus. I was trying not to make eye contact with him. It didn't work. He smiled an evil smile as he started down the aisle.

I slowly sank down into the seat. I knew he'd already seen me. I was hoping he'd take mercy on me since I was sitting with a couple of five-year-old kids. He stopped at my seat and slowly bent down. I knew he wanted to tell me something, so I slid closer to him. He looked around and whispered in my ear.

"Today must be your lucky day, kid," he said. He smiled and bumped into me as he walked to the back of the bus.

I was alive! I couldn't believe that was it. I had waited to be killed all day and that was it. *But what happened? What changed?*

I turned around and saw that he was counting something. I squinted and could see green—he was counting money. Someone had paid him off; someone had saved me!

-16-

We were a couple miles out of town when the bus radio went off again.

"Bus #21 and Bus #10, please turn around. I have Owen Nelson, Tommy Jones, and Jesse Hartel waiting in my office. They missed their buses," the radio blared.

I sat back and smiled. I couldn't believe it. No one had ever done anything nice for me, and I had just met these three today. I smiled all the way home. Pine Bluff might be a little town with only a couple stores, but there was something more to this little place. I couldn't explain it when I got home but didn't need to.

"How was your first day?" Mom quickly asked as I walked into the house.

"Great!" I said.

Both Mom and Dad stopped what they were doing and stared at each other. They both looked stunned.

I just smiled and walked back to my room. I dropped my book bag on my bed and walked over to turn on my video game system. Then I remembered that I still didn't have a controller, so I rested on my bed. Even the broken controller couldn't break my smile.

I racked my brain, trying to think of something to do to earn the money to buy the controller. It had been a couple days since I had played my video games, and I really missed it. Then I had an idea. I walked out to the kitchen.

"Hey, Mom, is there anything I can do around the house to earn a little extra money?" I asked.

"What do you need money for, honey?" Mom asked.

As I was going to answer her, Dad walked in.

"Is this about that video game controller?" he quickly asked.

"I need it, Dad. I can't play any of my games without it," I said.

With a frown, Dad asked, "Is that all you can think about? I told you before, Hunter, we don't have any extra money to worry about a video game controller you broke when you got mad. End of discussion!"

With that, Dad stormed out the front door. I knew we didn't have a lot of money, but I only needed fifty dollars. Dad had been looking for a new job since we moved to Pine Bluff, but there weren't many options in this small town.

I wanted to say something to my mom and tell her I wasn't being greedy, but I just walked back into my room.

What could I do? I had no video games for the first time in my life, and I had already explored the two-acre property on our little farm. That reminded me of the old newspapers.

I went over to my bed and knelt down, reaching

for the old box I had found. I grabbed the clippings and pulled them out. I started reading about all the things that had happened in Pine Bluff. Some of the papers were old, while others had been printed only a couple of years ago. There seemed to be no rhyme or reason as to why the person had collected the papers.

I found them interesting and started to learn a lot more about Pine Bluff. I read for about an hour and managed to get about halfway through the box. There were pictures of homecoming queens, the annual county fair, and other Pine Bluff events. Finally, my empty stomach got the best of me, and I went out to the kitchen table and sat down.

I'd smelled dinner cooking while I was reading. The aroma smelled like chicken and some type of rice, and I was starving. I'd been too nervous to eat breakfast, and I ha spent lunch hour at school hiding in the bathroom. I hadn't eaten in almost 24 hours.

Mom soon put the food on the table, and Dad joined us. It was quiet at first. I could tell I had hurt my dad's feelings. It was much deeper than my just wanting a video game—I had hurt my dad's pride. I knew he felt bad that he was jobless and couldn't afford to buy me a new video game controller.

After a few minutes, Dad spoke up. "Hunter, I know how much those silly games mean to you. I was hoping that this could be a new start for you—for all of us."

I started to feel worse. No longer was Dad angry; he just seemed sad. I wanted to say something but didn't know what to say. Even knowing all that, I still wanted that new controller.

"I think I have an idea of how you can get the money for a new controller," Dad said.

"Awesome! Anything, Dad. I'll do anything. If you need me to clean the car, the house—I'll do whatever I have to do," I said.

"That's good to hear, son, but the work won't be here. I was able to find you a part-time job—a job you can do after school to earn the extra money," said Dad.

"That's great, Dad!"

"There's one little catch, though."

"I don't care, Dad. At this point I'll do anything," I said enthusiastically.

"The job is helping a local farmer," Dad said.

"Farm? Okay, I don't know much about it, but I'll do my best," I said.

Dad's face changed, and he looked out the big bay windows facing the mountains. I ran over and gave him a hug.

"There's one more thing, Hunter. Your new job starts tomorrow, and it's with Kate."

-17-

"What? You got me a job working for that crazy woman? How could you do that? I can't work for her!"

Dad's face instantly changed, and I knew I shouldn't have said what I did.

"What did you just call her? Who are you to judge anyone, Hunter?" Dad said with his voice raised. "You need a job because you need money to buy a new controller. Now you have a way."

"Honey, he's right," Mom said.

I can't believe even Mom is on his side!

"I talked to her this afternoon," Dad continued, "and she said she needs some help on the farm. She was leery of giving you a chance, but I told her you were a fine worker."

I just sat there stunned. My day had been an emotional roller coaster. I went down, back up, and down again. I didn't have much of a choice. This was my only way to get the money for the controller. There was no way I could survive without my video game system.

But could I survive Crazy Kate? Everyone around town had told us how horrible she was. She lived up to her nickname. Now I was going to work for her!

That night I went to bed with a familiar feeling of fear. But this time I wasn't just afraid of a new school or a bully. I had an entirely different fear. I had already met the two roughest, toughest members of Pine Bluff. Up till now I had just been trying to think of ways to avoid Max. I hadn't even had time to worry about Crazy Kate.

After I got dressed the next morning, I pulled out an old Mason glass jar. In it, I had all the money I was saving. I originally was going to use the money to buy the new Fantasy Warrior game when it came out in November. I had only saved five dollars, but it was better than nothing. I wanted to at least have something to barter in case Max's bribe had run out.

I grabbed the five one-dollar bills, wadded them up, and stuck them in my pocket. In the kitchen I made some oatmeal and tried to eat breakfast but didn't have much of an appetite.

"Rough night last night, buddy? Mom asked.

"Where's Dad?" I asked.

"I don't know. He mentioned grabbing something for you—something from the old barn," Mom said.

Just as I was tying my shoes, the door opened. Dad walked in carrying something in his hand.

"Stones?" I asked.

Dad nodded and walked over to the kitchen table. He opened up his hands and slowly placed five stones on the table. Mom didn't say anything; she just kept on making his breakfast. Dad picked up one stone and placed it in my hand.

"Here, son, this is for you," he said.

I looked at him like he was crazy. *Had the thin mountain air gotten to my dad? Was he losing his mind?*

"Dad, what am I supposed to do with a stone?"

"These stones are special. Keep them in a safe place; you'll know what to use them for when the time is right," said Dad.

He walked over and grabbed a container from the cupboard and placed the remaining stones in it. He reached up to put the container on top of the refrigerator. I was still clueless.

I heard the loud horn of the bus approaching and saw the flashing light coming over the hill. I unzipped my backpack and slipped in the stone.

I took off running down the driveway to catch the bus. Just as I was getting on, I heard a loud sound coming off the mountain behind us.

It was his bugle; it was Boss. As we took off, I couldn't tell if the bus was shaking on its own or if Boss was bugling so loud he made it shake.

-18-

I sat down in the first seat—the one usually saved for kindergartners. *If I sit here every day, hopefully that will keep Max from tormenting me.*

The bus driver didn't say anything, so I slowly started to relax. The bumpy dirt road was soothing, and I started to drift off to sleep since I was still tired from the long night. Just as I was falling asleep, the bus brakes screeched to a halt.

A dust cloud engulfed us, and I rubbed my eyes to see where we were. Once the dust cleared, I could tell we were at Max's house. The driver beeped the horn twice. The whole bus held their breath, waiting for Max, but he didn't get on.

After what seemed like forever, the bus driver took off for the next stop. *Whew, no Max!* This day was looking good already. Maybe he had ridden to work with his dad. The rest of the route to school was pleasant, almost enjoyable. I noticed how the atmosphere in the bus changed—everyone was relieved that Max hadn't shown up.

We pulled in the Pine Bluff Elementary School parking lot. As I was about to step off the bus, I remembered something. My mom had given me a note to give to the driver about getting dropped off at Crazy Kate's house.

"Sorry, I almost forget this note," I said as I handed it to the driver.

I got off the bus, and after walking a couple feet, I heard the driver calling my name. I turned around and saw him waving me back to the bus.

"Is this note correct?" he asked. "This address… this is Crazy Kate's address."

"Yeah, it's correct. I'm going to be working for her after school for a couple of weeks," I answered.

His jaw dropped and he just stared at me. After

a long pause he looked up and said, "Okay, but I'm dropping you off at the corner. You can walk the rest of the way. I'm not going to go anywhere near her driveway."

Great. Not even the bus driver wanted to have a run in with Crazy Kate. I nodded and turned back towards the school. I was just about to open the doors when Owen, Jesse, and Tommy ran up.

"What's up, guys?" I asked.

"Hunter, you probably noticed that Max didn't ride the bus," Owen said.

I nodded and said, "Thanks a lot for yesterday. I really owe you guys."

"Don't mention it; I was new to Pine Bluff once too," Owen said.

Jesse spoke up, "Listen, don't mention anything to Mr. Wilson about Max not being here."

I was puzzled. *Wouldn't his dad know he wasn't here?*

"Trust me, his dad will think he's at school.

"We bought you one more day," Owen said with a wink.

Whatever it was, they had paid him enough money to keep me safe for two days!

"What am I going to do tomorrow?" I asked.

"Let's get through today. Let tomorrow worry about itself," said Owen.

I'm safe—at least for now. I had at least 24 hours before I'd have to see Max again.

The four of us walked in just as the bell was ringing. We went to our lockers and quickly started to put our belongings away.

"Good morning, boys," said Mr. Wilson.

"Morning, sir," Jesse said quickly.

Without missing a beat, Owen spoke up. "Mr. Wilson, can you please tell Max to leave me alone? He pushed me when he was walking into school."

Surprised, I glanced over at him. Mr. Wilson looked away nervously.

"No problem, I'll have a talk with him," Mr. Wilson muttered as he walked away.

I turned and looked at Owen.

"What are you doing? You lied to Mr. Wilson!" I exclaimed.

"Anytime you tell on Max, Mr. Wilson never does anything anyway. Now he'll for sure think Max is here. I never said what day he pushed me, so technically it's not lying," Owen said with a wink.

"Thanks, now it looks like I'll at least live until 3:00 p.m. today." I sighed.

"What do you mean? Max won't bother you today," Jesse said.

"It's not Max I'm worried about. Today I start a new job. After school I'm working for my neighbor," I said.

All three boys took a step back and stared at me. Their jaws were practically laying on the ground.

"Did you just say you're working for your neighbor? Your neighbor is Crazy Kate!" Tommy exclaimed.

"Yep, isn't that awesome? My dad talked to her because I need to earn money to buy a new video game controller," I told them sarcastically.

"Sorry, I can help you with Max, but you're on your own with Crazy Kate." Owen said, shaking his head.

-19-

With Max Wilson absent, school flew by, and I actually enjoyed it. I really liked getting to know Owen, Tommy, and Jesse. They were my friends now, and I loved having some real friends. The crazy thing was that they were total opposites of me—they were adventurous and loved to be outdoors. And the wildest thing was, they didn't even play video games! I couldn't believe I had friends who weren't gamers.

At lunch we talked about things we loved. I went on about my favorite game, Warrior's Challenge 13. They listened and were nice, but I could tell they had no interest in video games.

———

The boys told me about their families. They loved sports, especially hunting. They all shot bows together. Archery had always sounded cool to me, but I had never tried it.

The 3:00 p.m. bell finally rang, and again I wasn't excited about getting on the bus. Yesterday I feared the end of the day because of Max and today because I was going to Crazy Kate's house.

When the boys walked me to my bus, it felt like they were walking me to my funeral.

"Good luck today, Hunter. I hope I see you tomorrow. Just think—if you live through this, you'll have an awesome story to tell," Owen said.

I thanked them for the encouragement and boarded the bus. I started to daydream. We were only a couple miles outside of town when the bus suddenly screeched to a stop. It happened so fast it startled me and made me almost fly out of my seat.

Crossing in front of us were elk, and they were huge. I had never been so close to any before and couldn't believe how big they were! There were three females that a boy behind me said were called cows and one small bull. The bull had three points on one side and two on the other. The elk crossed the road, and Mr. Jenkins drove on like nothing had happened.

I started thinking about how I really wanted to explore the outdoors and go hunting like Owen and the rest of the guys. *But who will take me?* My dad didn't hunt—he had grown up in the city. His idea of hunting was to go outside and try to shoot some birds with an old BB gun. All that Dad knew about the outdoors was what he had learned from watching his collection of old Wild West movies.

"Hunter, your stop!" yelled the bus driver.

I tried to get up quickly, but it didn't work. The once lively and loud bus turned eerily quiet, almost like everyone was at a funeral. They all stared at me as I walked toward the front.

"Good luck, Hunter," said Mr. Jenkins.

I nodded reluctantly and walked off the bus. I could hear the crunching of the coarse gravel under my shoes. Mr. Jenkins floored the gas and sped off. He couldn't get away from Crazy Kate's fast enough. I turned to look at the big yellow bus as it turned into a huge dust cloud. Before I knew it, the bus had turned and was out of sight.

I only had about a two-hundred-yard walk from the corner to Kate's house, but I was taking as much time as I could. I was in no hurry to get there, plus I knew my dad was picking me up at six o'clock anyway. The less time I was there, the less I would have to be around Crazy Kate.

Crazy Kate's ranch was about 180 acres. There were some crops on the farm, but it was mostly livestock. She had a lot of animals. I remember hearing a story that she liked to talk to her animals. The weird part was she acted like the animals talked back. Other kids actually had heard her pretending that her animals were responding. Strange, just plain weird! It seemed like nothing was normal about my neighbor.

I walked down the driveway and into the front yard. I wasn't even sure where I was supposed to go. I knocked on the door, but there was no answer.

I went around to the barn and heard someone talking. I tiptoed closer and could hear Crazy Kate talking to her horse. I couldn't understand what she was saying, but it seemed like she was having a conversation with one of her horses.

I quietly stepped into the barn.

"Hello, Kate," I said.

She spun and stared. She leaned over and whispered something in the horse's ear.

"You're late!" she bellowed.

I just stood there and didn't know what to say.

"First things first, make sure you show up on time. I'm not paying you to be late. Second thing, every day when you get here, I want you to feed this horse. Her name is Scarlett. I also want you to feed my cat, Precious," Kate said.

I could handle that. I nodded and walked over to give Scarlett some hay.

"What are you doing, boy?" Kate demanded.

"I'm feeding the horse," I said.

"I told you her name is Scarlett. She isn't just a horse," Kate reminded me in an irritated way.

Then she added, "You were late, so I took the liberty of feeding her myself. Now go feed the cat!"

I scanned the room and looked, but there was no cat in sight. Kate could tell I was confused.

"The cat is in the house. You aren't the brightest light bulb, are you?" she said and sighed.

This woman was horrible and relentless. I walked out of the barn toward the back door of her house. Her house was old and showed lots of wear on the outside. It was really clean though, and I could tell she took a lot of pride in keeping it that way.

I walked in through the loud squeaking back screen door, and it made a huge banging sound as it flew shut behind me. There was no spring on it, so the door sounded like a cannon when it slammed shut.

The loud sound scared me, and I turned around to make sure Kate hadn't seen me jump in fear. Luckily, she must have still been in the barn. I went through the kitchen and into the main living room. I stared…I couldn't believe my eyes!

-20-

I was surrounded by animals! I looked around at the walls and saw these weren't barnyard animals. They were wild—at least they had been at one time. Her house was filled with animal mounts of all kinds, including deer, elk, and bear. Several mounts of huge elk that looked gigantic were above her fireplace.

I stood in awe for a couple minutes, wondering if anyone else knew about these treasures.

"See something you like, City Boy?" I heard a voice whisper behind me. I spun to see Crazy Kate a couple of feet away. *How did she make it past that old squeaking door without my hearing her?* I thought to myself.

"Wow, these are amazing!"

"Yep, and they're all mine. They eat good too," she said. "If you're done staring, maybe you should feed the cat like I told you to."

Kate pointed toward the corner of the room where there was a huge, cushioned bed and several bowls. I filled one bowl with water and the other with the gourmet cat food she had set out in the kitchen.

I turned and started admiring the mounts once again. I really liked the elk. Ever since I had heard one, I had been totally mesmerized by the big beast. Five elk heads lined one side of the wall. For some reason, there was a blank spot in the middle—like one was missing.

There were so many other mounts. Then I saw a cool cat—I guessed it was a stuffed bobcat—sitting on the table near the window. I walked over to get a closer look when, all of a sudden, it moved!

I lurched back. Crazy Kate started laughing.

"Come here, Precious, it's time to eat. City Boy got you some food and water."

Precious was huge—by far the biggest cat I had ever seen. She was pitch-black and must have weighed at least thirty pounds. I felt really stupid when I realized it was her pet and not a mounted bobcat.

"My name is actually Hunter," I stuttered.

She looked at me and laughed, actually it was more of a cackle.

"I know your name, boy; I ain't dumb. But I'm going to call you City Boy," Kate said.

Whatever—as long as you pay me, I thought.

"Why is there an open spot by the other elk?" I asked.

"Shut up and mind your own business," Kate snapped back.

Just before she walked out the door, she turned and looked at me.

"City Boy, grab the pitchfork. There's some pig manure that needs to be shoveled," she said with a smile.

I watched Crazy Kate walk back out of the house toward the barn. She had an unmistakable limp; her right leg didn't work right.

I spent the next two hours shoveling pig manure and adding straw. I couldn't wait for 6:00 p.m. This was the longest two-and-a-half hours of my life. I smelled horrible, and I was completely exhausted. I hadn't seen Crazy Kate since she had showed me exactly how she wanted the pig stalls done.

I felt like crying, but I didn't want to give her something else to tease me about. I also didn't want her to think I was a wimp.

I heard the loud exhaust of a car pull in and felt relieved to see my dad walk into the barn.

"Okay, Hunter, it's 6:00 p.m. Time to go, son."

I walked over and set the pitchfork down. I wanted to wipe the sweat off my forehead but thought I should wait until I got home and washed my hands. They were filthy.

Just as we were walking out, I heard the loud slam of the back screen door. I turned and saw Crazy Kate coming toward us. Had she been inside the entire time I was working? She slammed the door on purpose; it was obvious that she wanted it to be heard. I bet she sat in her house watching me, laughing at me. I started to boil.

"Hold on! Before you go, let me pay you," she said.

I perked up a little bit. At least I was going to have some cash for all my hard work. I'd be one step closer to buying that video game controller.

"Here you go, your pay for today. I'll pay you every day in case you decide you're gonna quit on me," she said as she handed me some bills.

I looked down and counted them quickly. *Five dollars?* She had only paid me five dollars for almost three hours of back-breaking work? I couldn't believe it!

I tried to hide my reaction because I didn't want to seem ungrateful. But five dollars wouldn't even pay for the cardboard box the controller came in.

She looked at me and grinned, almost like she was testing me, wanting me to complain. I was sure Dad even thought she was being cheap.

"Thanks, Kate. You'll see him right after school tomorrow," Dad added.

He added, "Son, don't you have something to say to Miss Kate?"

I was fuming. I was so mad. There were a million things I wanted to say to this miserable, old hag. I had to be careful. I couldn't let my temper get the best of me, but I also couldn't let her make a mockery of all my hard work.

"Thanks. I'll see you tomorrow, *Crazy* Kate," I muttered.

-21-

My dad gasped and glared at me. I knew I made a big mistake as soon as I had said it.

"Get in the car NOW!" he yelled.

I knew why he was angry. He had told me from day one never to call her Crazy Kate. But I was so mad at her, I wanted to hurt her and get her back for all the things she had done to me. I thought I had every right to because she deserved it.

I saw my dad talking with Crazy Kate, and she didn't look happy. After a couple of minutes, Dad came back to the car. I just wanted to get out of there. At this point, no matter what I said or did wasn't going to be right.

Dad got in and started the car. I kept waiting for him to say something, to tell me what my punishment would be. *What's the worse thing he can do? Take away my video games? Too late, I'm already without them.* We were only in the car for about two minutes or so because it was a short drive from Crazy Kate's ranch to our little farmhouse.

So far all that I was getting from my dad was silence. This was worse than being yelled at. I didn't know what he was going to say. As we pulled into the house, the car slowly came to a stop. Dad put the car in park and looked me directly in the eyes.

"How could you?" he asked in a bitter tone.

"She deserved it! How could I? Dad, do you know what she put me through today? For five bucks?" I yelled back.

I was starting to lose my temper. I was sick of it, sick of all of it—broken video game controller, a huge bully on the bus, and a crazy neighbor tormenting me. I had reached my breaking point; I was at my wit's end.

Then Dad did something that totally surprised

me. Without saying a word, he opened the car door and walked into the house. I didn't know what to do, but I knew this conversation wasn't over. I sat there for a minute looking off into the mountains, justifying the way I felt toward Crazy Kate. I sat in our old Buick talking to myself. I was going through the entire list of reasons why I hated Crazy Kate and had the right to call her names.

What's the big deal? Everyone called her names, so she was used to it. In fact, she had probably earned them. She didn't try to prove anyone wrong. She lived up to her nickname every time she encountered someone.

I was about to open the car door and head toward the house when I saw our front door open. Dad came over and opened my door, holding something in his hand. I got out and stared at him, waiting for him to yell at me.

He opened his hand and silently handed me another stone. I just stood there, holding my second stone as Dad turned around and walked back into the house.

I didn't know what he was trying to prove with these stupid stones. But I was still angry, so I just bent down and added it to the other stone in my backpack. To be honest, I wanted to take out the stones and throw them at Crazy Kate. But I was pretty sure that wasn't why Dad kept giving them to me. Shaking my head, I got out of the car and headed to the house.

Looking up at the sky, I stopped short. Despite all the drama I had just encountered, the western sunset will stop anyone in their tracks. I couldn't help but admire the creation that was around us. I was mad but somehow the sunset took away some of that anger. I just stood in awe, watching the mountain glow from the sun.

After a couple minutes, I went to the front door. I desperately needed a hot shower and some food. I'd never worked that hard in my life. Just as I turned the doorknob, I heard him! There was a mighty bugle—one that had to be the huge bull elk Owen told me about.

His bugle sent shivers down my spine. He was

Boss, the dominant bull, the master of the mountain, and I was just a smelly city boy who was trying to survive the wilds of Colorado.

And so far, I was losing.

-22-

Mom didn't say much during dinner and neither did Dad. The shower had felt great, but I could still smell Crazy Kate's pigs. I didn't know if the smell was from my boots near the front door or if it was still lingering on me. I couldn't seem to get the odor off me.

After dinner I said goodnight. I was going to bed early; I was completely exhausted. The manual labor combined with the drama from Crazy Kate's was enough to send me there well before my usual bedtime. Plus, I hadn't slept well all week.

I was tired but not sleepy tired. I rolled over a couple times, trying to get comfortable. My body ached, but my mind was racing. I finally gave up and got up. Since I couldn't play any of my video games, I dug out the old box of newspaper clippings again. I spent some time reading and learning more about Pine Bluff. Most of the articles were about common things and sports, but every once in a while, I'd find an article that was really interesting and read it.

My favorite was about the time when a presidential candidate had visited Pine Bluff. The article said the streets were packed with over 300 people filling the town to welcome the President. I had to laugh; there were more than 300 kids just in my grade back in Denver.

I pulled out a jar from my dresser that I had tucked inside of one of my long, black socks. I pulled the money out of my pocket and added it to my collection. I now had ten dollars to my name, so I was a little closer to buying the video game controller. I still needed another forty dollars.

Just as I was nodding off to sleep, I remembered my other problem—Max. He would be back in school tomorrow. The money my buddies had paid him only gave me a two-day break.

I had to come up with a plan and fast. The last thing I wanted was to get beat up on the bus tomorrow morning. *But what can I do?* It was starting to get late, and I was so tired. I drifted off to sleep, thinking of ways to avoid Max tomorrow.

I heard my mom's voice waking me up.

"Hunter, you need to wake up, honey. It's late. I let you sleep in," she said.

"What?" I mumbled.

"Honey, I let you sleep in because you were so tired. But now you need to get ready or you're going to be late," said Mom.

Late? Of all mornings to be late. I hadn't come up with a plan for Max yet. I jumped up and scrambled for my clothes. I was in a panic as I stumbled around my room. I raced over and grabbed the ten dollars from my dresser and stuffed it into my pocket. I looked out and saw the bus sitting at the end of my driveway. I took off running toward the front door.

"Hunter, slow down. I'll take you to school today," said Dad.

Whew! I took a deep breath. At least I had a way of avoiding Max this morning.

"Come over and eat," Dad said.

I went over to the table. Now that my dad was taking me, I actually had time to eat before heading to school. After breakfast, we loaded up in the car and drove off. Ours was a quiet ride. Dad and I hadn't talked much since the incident yesterday with Crazy Kate.

When we pulled into the school parking lot, Dad put the car into park.

"Hunter, you need to ride the bus to Kate's house after school," Dad said.

I nodded and thanked my dad for the ride.

"Oh, one more thing, son," Dad said as he reached into his coat pocket.

I stuck out my hand, hoping he was giving me some lunch money or something important. He opened his hand and handed me another stone.

I looked at him with a puzzled look. Dad could

tell I was still clueless, but out of respect, I took the third stone from him.

I waved as Dad drove off and bent down to add the third stone to my backpack collection. I turned to see kids getting off the buses. I had to hurry. I wanted to beat them into school so I could avoid Max. I wasn't quick enough and saw a huge dark shadow moving behind me. I was alone in the school parking lot with no adults and no sign of Owen, Jesse, and Tom. I had to think fast, but what could I do? Max was heading toward me, and he looked mad.

I did the only thing I could think of. I reached down and unzipped my backpack, looking for something to grab, anything to defend myself.

My hand felt something cold and hard. It was one of the stones that my dad had given me. I stood up with the stone in my hand. Maybe I should throw this at Max. I could use this stone to protect me from the giant who was approaching. My dad was an avid reader of the Bible, and one of his favorite stories was David and Goliath. I remember sitting in my Sunday school class back in Denver and learning about the heroic story.

Maybe he knew about the bully and wanted to give me something to defend myself from Max. He was close.

Max shouted, "You're going to die, City Boy!"

What is it with these people calling me City Boy? The name calling was starting to drive me nuts.

Max was about twenty feet away and closing fast. My mind was racing. I reached back with the stone and threw it as hard as I could.

-23-

As soon as I let it go, I knew it was a mistake. In no way would my dad approve of my throwing stones at a bully. I watched as the stone sailed toward Max. Everything was moving in slow motion, and I wish I could have stopped it.

Max ducked to his right, and thankfully the stone sailed past him and fell harmlessly to the ground. I thought he was mad before, but now he was furious.

"You trying to kill me or something, City Boy?" Max yelled as started jogging toward me.

I braced myself for some type of punch or kick. I closed my eyes and waited for impact. Max stopped so close I could smell his terrible breath. I slowly opened my eyes, and the bully was inches away from my face, glaring at me.

"Your boys saved you for two days, but the bank is empty. I'm back now, and that's not good news for you," Max said.

Just then I reached into my back pocket as my last resort.

Max stepped back and warned, "You better not be reaching for another stone."

I slowly flashed the ten dollars I'd been saving for my new video game controller. "How much? How much will it cost me for you to leave me alone?" I asked.

"How much you got?" he demanded.

I gently pulled all the one-dollar bills and counted it in front of him.

"One week—that will give you one week of peace. But if I were you, I'd find some more money fast because it will cost you a lot more next time," Max said as he grabbed the ten dollars and walked toward the school.

For a second, I thought about grabbing my second stone and hurling it at his head but thought that probably wasn't the best idea. I went over and picked up the stone that I'd thrown.

Stupid stone, a lot of good you did, I thought.

I unzipped my backpack and added it to the other two. I'd bought myself some freedom, but I knew it was only temporary. I walked into school late and tried sneaking through the main hallway to my class.

"Going somewhere, Hunter?" I heard a voice call out.

I turned and saw Mr. Wilson standing there, and next to him was Max. For a second, I thought Max had told him I'd thrown a stone at him. I saw Mr. Wilson writing out something and handing it to Max.

"Thanks, Dad," Max said with a smile as he turned and started walking to class. I could see the piece of paper in his hands, and now it was obvious that it was a hall pass.

"Why are you late, Hunter?" Mr. Wilson asked.

Whew! Max hadn't said anything, which made sense since he had my money.

"I had a rough morning," I quickly said.

"We all have those, don't we, son?" Mr. Wilson said as he was writing something.

I was relieved, thinking he was giving me a hall pass for being tardy.

"Give this to Mr. Peavey. Tomorrow make sure you're on time," Mr. Wilson said. He quickly added, "One more thing, Hunter. I know you live on Redemption Road. I don't know if you know this or not, but there is rumored to be a huge elk over there. Have you seen any big bull elk?"

I had to think fast, and I knew lying wasn't an option. My parents always taught me that lying was never okay, and I believed them.

"I haven't seen any big bulls behind our house, sir," I quickly answered.

"Well, if you do, let me know. That kind of stuff interests me," he said.

I technically wasn't lying. He had asked me if I had seen any bulls, and I hadn't—I had only heard him. He handed me the piece of paper, and I walked to class and handed Mr. Peavey the paper.

"That's too bad, Hunter. You're in lunch detention today for being tardy," he said.

I had already guessed it wasn't a hall pass.

-24-

Mr. Wilson had given me a detention, but he had given Max a hall pass. I wasn't too surprised and knew this was going to be a tough battle.

At lunch, Owen, Jesse, and Tommy were asking me all kinds of questions about Max, Mr. Wilson, and Crazy Kate. I told them the whole story—even the part about throwing the stone at Max.

"I'm not surprised, Hunter. Mr. Wilson is always bailing Max out; he never gets in trouble. I know why Mr. Wilson is asking you about Boss," said Owen. "He's a huge hunter, and everyone around town has heard about Boss."

"Why don't they hunt him then?" I asked. "He

seemed like he wasn't hiding from anyone. I've heard him bugle several times just in the short time that I've lived there."

Jesse spoke up, "Boss is on Crazy Kate's property, Hunter, so no one can get to him. That's part of the reason why he's so huge. He's been a legend around Pine Bluff the past couple of years. People have tried to get close, but no one can, and they don't want to risk their lives by trespassing on her land."

"But Kate hunts; why doesn't she shoot him?" I asked.

"She probably will this year. Now that the bull is record-book size, she'll go after him. I heard she really wants to add him to her collection," said Owen.

Her collection was fantastic. It was all beginning to make sense. The spot that was open on her wall between the other animals was reserved for Boss.

"We need to come up with a plan for Max," Tommy said.

"How much time did you buy?" Owen asked.

"One week," I told them.

We had one week to think of a way to get Max off my back. I couldn't afford to keep paying off this kid. At this rate I'd never be able to buy my video game controller.

Lunch detention was boring, and I missed being outside with my friends. Five other kids were in detention, and I wondered if they were in there because of Max too.

The rest of the day flew by, and soon I was on the bus ready to head for Crazy Kate's. I took my seat and stared out the window. Max got on the bus and walked right past me. He pushed some kids out of nearby seats before sitting in his regular spot at the back of the bus.

At least he's leaving me alone.

As I thought about that for a minute, I decided maybe it was the best ten dollars I had ever spent. But then I remembered how hard I'd worked for that money. It wasn't fair that Max treated people this way and got away with it.

The bus stopped at the corner and let me off. I walked a little faster than I had yesterday. I didn't feel like hearing Crazy Kate yell at me for being late and calling me *City Boy*.

This time I went right to the barn and started feeding Scarlett. At first there was no sign of Kate, so I went into the house to feed Precious. Usually when I went into the house, the huge cat was waiting to greet me. I figured that the cat could hear the loud screen door closing.

I was still amazed at how big Precious was. I was also surprised that Crazy Kate fed her expensive gourmet cat food. She paid more for the cat's food than she paid me to work on the farm.

I walked around, looking for Crazy Kate to see what she wanted me to do next. I searched around the entire barnyard but couldn't find her. I went back toward the house.

I opened the door and used my back foot to close it slowly, so there was no slamming noise this time. As I walked in, I could hear Crazy Kate talking to Precious.

"It's okay, Precious, I'm going to get you some help soon. I'm so sorry, baby," she said.

When I neared them, I noticed Precious wasn't quite herself.

"Miss Kate, is something wrong with Precious?" I asked.

Crazy Kate was startled that I had snuck up on her, but I could tell her thoughts were on Precious.

"What do you care, City Boy?" she asked. Her voice was different; it was sad.

"I was just wondering," I said.

"She's sick and is getting worse," Crazy Kate finally muttered.

She added, "I'm not paying you to stare at Precious. Go and shovel out the chicken coop."

First pigs and now chickens. I knew it wasn't a coincidence that they were two of the smelliest animals on the farm. I wished she'd have me take Scarlett for a walk or feed the cows, but not for this city boy. She was going to have me do the most disgusting jobs on the farm.

At 6:00 p.m. Dad pulled in and saved me from

Crazy Kate's farm. This time, she was already outside and walked over toward us. She handed me five crumpled dollar bills and walked back in the house.

This time I kept my mouth shut.

-25-

"How's it going on Kate's farm?" Mom asked at dinner.

I looked at Dad. I wasn't sure how to respond—if I should be honest or polite.

"Fine," I said.

"She sure is a unique woman, isn't she?" Mom asked.

"Unique is one way to put it," I responded.

"You should be thankful, Hunter. I know she's getting older and having trouble keeping up with the farm. She doesn't have enough money to hire full-time help," Mom said.

Everyone knew she didn't have a lot of money.

In fact, I don't know if I had ever seen her leave her property.

"Where does she buy her groceries?" I asked.

"She doesn't buy a lot, tries to raise most it. She hunts for her food and lives most of the year off the meat. Would you leave your house much if people talked about you the way they talk about Kate?" Mom asked.

She has a good point. Wherever we went, people would say something really bad about Crazy Kate. I knew she was a good hunter, especially after seeing her trophy room. I'm sure she filled her freezer with lots of elk and deer meat.

"You know, Hunter, there might be more to our neighbor than you can see," Dad said.

Even so I was still not going to feel sorry for her. The way she treated people was wrong, and I'm the one who had to deal with her every day.

"I guess, but she doesn't help herself much with the way she treats people," I said.

"Well, Hunter, I guess you can only control how you treat people," said Mom.

"I suppose so," I said.

After dinner, we played a game of Monopoly, my favorite game. The three of us loved to play it. I think one reason was because it made us feel like we had money—like we could own Park Place and Boardwalk. My dad always seemed to buy both of those properties. Even though it was paper money, we all felt rich when we played.

Mom actually won, but it took her a couple or hours before she made me go bankrupt. After we put the game away, I went into the bathroom to brush my teeth, and Dad went over to the couch and started watching an old western.

One of the cowboys caught my attention right away. He walked with such confidence, and when he spoke, people listened. I was intrigued by this cowboy. I admired everything about him, especially his beat-up Stetson hat. It looked a lot like the one that I'd found in the old barn.

After a couple of minutes, I said goodnight and went into my bedroom. I pulled out the old box of newspapers and started reading again.

After a couple minutes, I was down to the last newspaper at the bottom of the box. I pulled it out and read the date. Though it had been printed twenty years ago, it was still one of the more recent newspapers in the pile. I scanned the headlines, and one instantly caught my eye: "Three Die in Redemption Road Wreck." I quickly read the photo caption:

A recent crash claimed the lives of three Pine Bluff family members on December 24. The crash took the lives of Jeff Patterson and his 14-year-old son Zack and 10-year-old daughter, Morgan. Katherine Patterson, the wife and mother, suffered a broken leg but was stabilized.

I ran out of my room and into the living room.

"Dad, what did you say Kate's last name was?" I quickly asked.

"Patterson. Why, Son?" Dad replied.

-26-

I held up the article and showed my parents.
"Sit down, Son," Dad said.

I could tell right away that they both had known about the accident. Dad got up and walked over to the refrigerator and brought down the container holding the stones. He grabbed a stone and walked over. He set the stone down in front of me. "Let he who is without sin cast the first stone," said Dad.

That's when it all made sense. I knew my dad was referencing a verse from the Bible—from the book of John.

I knew I had been wrong about the way I had looked at Kate and the way I thought about her.

Thinking back to the first time I had heard her name at the pizza restaurant, my mind had already been made up. Sure, she seemed mean, but I didn't really know her. It wasn't my job to judge her or anyone else.

I sat and listened to my parents with a huge lump in my throat. They told me more about the accident that had left Katherine Patterson a widow. At first the townspeople had helped her and supported her, but over time her heart turned cold and so did the people in Pine Bluff.

Had people forgotten about the crash? Did Kate's attitude turn people from her? I was practically speechless, and I knew I wasn't innocent. I had talked badly about Kate and bought into what everyone else had been saying about her.

"Son, remember you can only control how you treat people. You can't control how they treat you. But when you go to sleep at night, after you say your prayers, make sure you can sleep," said Dad.

I decided to keep the stones in my backpack as a reminder.

I went to my room and dug out the old cowboy hat I'd found in the barn. I slipped it into my backpack. I knew what Dad meant; he didn't need to say another word. I couldn't get Miss Kate off my mind, so I tried thinking of something I enjoyed.

My first thought was about playing video games, but for some reason that didn't satisfy me anymore.

The next morning was uneventful. Max was nowhere in sight. He was sticking to our deal. I couldn't believe it was only Thursday. So much had changed in my first week at Pine Bluff.

I was different in a lot of ways—a good different, I think. Besides having friends and a job, both which were firsts for me, I hadn't played any video games since I had broken my controller.

The bell finally rang for first recess. Our class raced out the doors and were delighted to see a light October snow on the ground.

Owen looked at me and said, "This will be great for elk hunting! The snow will push the herd down from the mountains."

Elk season in Colorado is a big deal—a really

big deal actually. Hunting is a rich tradition and provided locals with food for the rest of the year.

"Do you think Mr. Wilson is going to win the annual Elk Pole again?" Tommy asked.

"Elk Pole? What's that?" I asked.

"Every year Garner's Grocery Store runs an elk-hunting contest. The winner wins a $250 gift card to the grocery store, but more important, bragging rights around Pine Bluff," said Jesse.

"For the past three years, Mr. Wilson has won. He takes it really seriously. He has to always win—always get the biggest bull," Owen added.

"Besides the gift card, the winner gets a huge trophy and their picture on the front page of the newspaper," Tommy added.

"Maybe he won't win this year," I said.

"I doubt it. He already registered a huge 6 x 6 bull elk at the store this past weekend. It looks like it could go into the county record books. The contest ends Saturday at noon," Owen said.

"The contest ends this weekend at noon—high noon," I said with a smile. *"Hmmm…"*

-27-

It was strange; I had never even hunted, but I knew Boss was bigger than the one Mr. Wilson had bagged. I felt it in my gut; I felt it every time I heard his bugle. I had no doubt that he was the most majestic beast, the head of his herd. He was the boss of the entire mountain—an elk that would win the Garner's Grocery Store Elk Pole.

"Yeah, but that isn't even an option; no one is going to kill that elk. No one is going to go on Crazy Kate's property," Owen said.

As soon as he said it, it bothered me. It was different this time, different than the thousands of times I'd said it.

"I'd appreciate it if you would call her Kate or Miss Kate," I said.

"Huh?! Is she starting to grow on you or something?" Tommy asked.

"Something," I replied.

I added, "What has she ever done to any of you? Have you ever even talked to her?"

I watched the three boys as they looked as each other. Finally, Owen spoke up.

"You know, you're right, Hunter. I've never even met her."

"Exactly! So who are we to judge?"

I didn't want to go into detail about the car crash. I finally figured out why my parents hadn't told me. They didn't want me to be nice to Kate just because of her tragedy. They wanted me to be nice to her because it was right to do.

We all put our hands together and made an oath. From now on she was going to be Miss Kate.

"There's a way to knock Mr. Wilson off that elk leaderboard and crown a new champion in Pine Bluff," I said.

"How?" Jesse asked.

"Kate can win," I replied.

Now I had to find a way to convince her to pursue Boss. Miss Kate needed to win the Elk Pole. She needed the gift card more than anyone else, and I didn't want to see Mr. Wilson win.

This bus ride to Miss Kate's was much different than the other ones. I had a lot on my mind. I didn't fear her or have any hate in my heart for her anymore. I knew what I needed to do, and even though it was going to be hard, I was going to do it.

This time when I got off the bus, I started jogging toward Miss Kate's ranch. I didn't have a lot of time to waste. Sunday was the last day in October before the elk contest ended.

First, I started feeding Scarlett and made sure she had ample food and water. Next, I moved into the house to take care of Precious. I walked into the storage room to get Precious a can of her gourmet food. I grabbed it and turned around.

"You're early!" Miss Kate said surprised.

"I am; this time I ran when I got off the bus."

Miss Kate halfway smiled.

"Now if you would have done that in the beginning, you would have been on time every day."

She was right. I had done everything possible to avoid working on her ranch, and she had noticed it. Maybe there was a method to her madness.

"Miss Kate, there's something I need to tell you," I said.

"You ain't quitting on me, are you?" she asked in a low voice.

"I'm sorry," I said.

Miss Kate stopped and stared at me. She wasn't sure what to say.

"Whatcha sorry for?" she asked.

-28-

"I'm sorry for calling you that name the other night," I said.

"Is that all, City Boy? People call me names all the time," she said.

"Yeah, but I shouldn't. And for that I'm sorry," I said.

Miss Kate's body language started to change. I couldn't tell if she was happy or mad; I don't think she knew how to respond.

Then I did something I never thought in a million years I would do. I walked over and hugged Miss Kate. She felt so cold, but she didn't pull away from me. She embraced me back but only for a second. When she stepped back, I saw her wipe away a tear.

"Thanks. Now get out and take care of those chickens. The pen is still a mess," she said.

I didn't want to bring up the hurt from the accident and didn't need to. Knowing about the accident had helped change my heart. She had been through enough pain.

At 6:00 p.m. Miss Kate came out to the chicken coop and handed me five more dollars.

"Thanks, but that's all the work I'll be needing you for," she said.

"But why? I'm doing better. I'll work harder tomorrow, I promise," I said.

"It's not that, boy, you're doing just fine. I just can't have you here working for a while, that's all."

Dad pulled up in the car and motioned for me to come.

"See ya later, Kate," Dad yelled out from the window as we drove off toward home.

I was confused. I was just starting to like working on Miss Kate's ranch.

When we pulled in our driveway, Dad said, "Son, your mom and I have a little surprise for you in the house."

Is he trying to cheer me up? Did he know that this was going to be my last day of work? At this point, it didn't matter. Ever since arriving at Pine Bluff I had nothing but surprises, and most of them weren't good ones. Hoping it was a good surprise, I took off out of the car as fast as I could and hit the front door running. Mom was waiting for me.

"It's in your room," she said. I raced down the hallway and opened my bedroom door. A wrapped box was sitting on my desk. I ripped it open. It was a new video game controller! I was thrilled, but how did they afford it? I turned around and saw Mom and Dad waiting for me in the kitchen.

"Hunter, we're so proud of how hard you've been working this past week. We wanted to do something special for you," Mom said.

"But we don't have extra money for this kind of stuff," I protested.

"Your dad and I had a little bit saved up from

the sale of our furniture. Don't worry about it, son; just enjoy it."

"We actually bought it Tuesday but wanted you to earn it. And I think you have," added Dad.

I was still trying to process everything. I had a new controller and still had a little money I had earned from working at Miss Kate's. My first thought was to use the money to pay off Max for another couple of weeks.

"There's something else I need to tell you. It's about Kate and working on her farm," Dad said.

"What about it?" I asked.

"I actually set the whole thing up with Kate. I asked her to let you help, and I even gave her the money to pay you each day. I figured it would be a good lesson. Kate doesn't have the money to pay for help; that's why it ended today," Dad said.

At first, I wasn't quite sure how to act. I had learned a great lesson this week about Miss Kate but even more importantly about myself. I stood there, trying to process everything that had just happened. Then I knew what I had to do.

———

"Do you still have the receipt for the video game controller?" I asked.

"Of course, why?" Mom asked.

"Because we need to return it!" I declared.

-29-

"I'm sorry; you lost me. You want us to *return* the controller?" Dad asked.

"Yeah, and I want you to take all my video game stuff and sell it to Vince's Movie Rental uptown. I saw an ad in the paper saying they buy used video game equipment," I said.

"We don't need money that bad. Just keep it; you earned it," Mom said.

"Sorry, but the money isn't for you," I said.

They could tell that I was serious. Mom started to ask more questions and tried to convince me to keep the controller. As she was talking to me, I walked over to my backpack and pulled out the stones. I walked over and handed them back to my dad. "Dad, I don't need these anymore," I said with a smile.

Dad nodded and smiled back. He looked at my mom and raised his hand to let her know to let the matter drop.

We sat down, and I explained to them what I had been thinking about. We hatched out a plan that I was sure would work. They were going to take the controller back and sell my video game equipment to the local video store in nearby Craig. Then they would put the money in the envelope and leave it in Miss Kate's mailbox so I could grab it after school.

When I went to bed that night, for the first time in a long time I had a peaceful night's sleep.

The next morning, I was up before my alarm and actually waiting outside for the bus. I was ready to finish this week, but today was going to be special.

I was on a mission.

The bus was running a little behind, and it was

a chilly October morning. A little bit of snow was still covering the ground.

I could hear the bus coming before I could see it. Sounds travel and echo through our valley, and the sound of that old bus was unmistakable. It came to a stop in front of my house.

The bus was stopped, but for some reason, I still heard a loud sound. It wasn't the bus; it was Boss, and he was calling to me.

"You just stay around here, big guy," I whispered as I got on the bus.

I was slowly starting to enjoy my morning bus rides through the back country of Pine Bluff. In fact, I was loving my new life. If you would have told me a week ago when we were traveling from Denver that I was going to be selling my video game equipment, I would have told you that you were crazy. But something had changed; something was different. Something was better; for the first time I was happy being me.

The bus pulled into the school and started to unload. I was pretty happy as I headed into the school. There was a buzz going around. Everyone seemed excited and ready for the weekend. I had just turned the corner to the sixth-grade hallway when I felt a hand grab me and pull me into the janitor's closet. It was Owen.

"I'm so glad I found you. Did you ride the bus?" he asked.

"Yeah, why?" I asked.

"Was Max on it?" he quickly asked. Now that he mentioned it, I hadn't seen Max on the bus that morning.

"No, he wasn't," I replied.

"Well, he's at school, and he's looking for you," Owen declared.

"Why is he looking for me?" I asked. I hadn't talked to him or had any problems with him since I had paid him the ten dollars on Tuesday.

"Yesterday during gym class, my brother heard him talking to a couple of his friends. He said he was sick of 'this new city kid,' and he planned on taking care of him in front of the whole school to-morrow."

"But that's today," I said.

"I know, I'm just glad I got to you first. You need to go to the office and call home; tell them you're sick," Owen warned me.

I thought for a minute or so. This news had thrown me for a loop. I wasn't expecting any problems with Max today. I turned and looked at Owen.

"This ends today—follow me!" I said.

I unzipped my backpack and pulled out the old cowboy hat that I'd found in the barn.

"What in the world are you doing, Hunter?" Owen asked.

I flipped on the old Stetson hat and started strutting down the main hall toward Max. I felt like one of those old cowboys from my dad's movies. The once loud hallway was quiet, and everyone stopped as I walked toward the bully. I shouted, "Max Wilson!"

I thought Owen was going to fall over dead in his boots. Kids started circling us and chanting, "Fight! Fight!"

Max looked around; he couldn't believe some

new city kid had called him out in front of the whole school. He got a huge grin—the kind that says "I'm gonna kill ya."

He dropped the freshman kid he was shoving into his locker and started walking toward me.

"You're gonna die, City Boy!"

-30-

I pulled down the brim of my hat and stared directly at Max as he was walking toward me. When I put that hat on, I felt like someone else. I had pictured myself as an old cowboy, trying to tame the Wild West.

"Take off that hat, City Boy," Max yelled.

I stood my ground and looked him square in the eyes. On the inside I was terrified, but I had to look tough. I tried to look like Clint Eastwood or John Wayne.

"You want a fight? You lookin' for trouble, are ya?" I asked in my toughest voice.

Max started laughing. "Who are you supposed

to be? Some dork cowboy? I'm going to pound you!" Max yelled.

By now our modest crowd had grown into a much larger one. I even saw some teachers and other staff members watching to see what was going to happen next.

"You think you're so tough, Wilson, but you're not. You're nothing but a spoiled brat!" I yelled back at him.

When I said it, the onlookers gasped so loud the hallway echoed. Max looked around.

I added, "I'll meet you at high noon tomorrow, and this time your daddy can't save you."

By now the bully was in angry overload, and his face was as red as a tomato. I was hoping and praying he didn't turn my face into mashed potatoes right then.

"Done! Just name the place, City Boy!"

"Elk Pole," I bellowed back.

I looked him square in the eyes. "You aren't scared, are ya?" I asked.

"I'll be there!" he yelled.

"You better be!" I shouted.

I turned and slowly walked away. Everyone gathered in the hallway was in shock. The last thing I heard was Max yelling, "Noon on Saturday! You better be there!"

Owen walked with me, and his jaw was almost dragging the ground.

"Dude, what in the world are you doing?"

-31-

The whole school was abuzz about my show-down with Max. I had gained instant celebrity status in the sixth grade. During recess, I bet I signed twenty autographs for a bunch of elementary school kids, most of whom had all fallen victim to Max. Some thought I wouldn't be back in school on Monday and wanted a souvenir.

Owen, Tommy, and Jesse pulled me aside during lunch to try to reason with me.

"What are you thinking, Hunter? There's no way you can fight Max," Tommy said.

Jesse jumped in, "Why did you do that in front of everyone? Now the whole school will be there!"

"I sure hope so. I hope the whole town comes out to see it," I said.

"Hunter, what in the world is going on? You're not making sense. Please tell me you have a plan," Owen begged.

Of course, I had a plan, but I had to be careful how much I told anyone. I trusted these three, but people were everywhere, and I couldn't take the risk.

"Trust me. You'll want to be there to witness it in person. I'll fill you in later about my plan—I just don't want to do it here," I said with a grin.

That seemed to calm them down for a little while. The rest of the day I was getting high fives and thumbs up from everyone in school—even kids in the high school wing at Pine Bluff.

It seemed like I wasn't the only one who wanted to see Max pay. I was just the only one seemingly dumb enough to take action.

By the time the bell rang at the end of the day, everyone knew about the fight that was taking place tomorrow at noon. And that was exactly the way

I wanted it. When I went to the bus to go home, everyone cheered. I felt like a celebrity. Thankfully, Max had wrestling practice and didn't ride the bus home. Even the bus driver wished me good luck.

-32-

The bus was almost to the corner of Redemption Road—the place where I had been dropped off all week. This time the bus didn't stop; the driver turned and started traveling down Redemption Road and came to a screeching halt in front of Miss Kate's ranch. *I can't believe it!* For the first time the driver had taken me right up to her driveway.

I headed toward the front of the bus to get off.

"Thanks a lot," I said as I passed the driver.

He nodded and then grabbed my arm. "Good luck, Hunter," he said.

Even he knew about the big showdown. Word travels fast in a small town. I thought this was his way of showing me that he was proud of me, proud that someone had finally stood up to Max Wilson.

I waved as the bus drove away and quickly took off across the road to the mailbox. I pulled down the steel door and grabbed the envelope of cash my parents had dropped off. I stood there in the road and counted it slowly. There was over $300 in the envelope, so I knew that all my video game equipment was gone.

As soon as my feet hit the gravel driveway, I sprinted toward the barn. I fed Scarlett and ran toward the house. I didn't have much time to spare. I flew in and heard the banging sound of the screen door behind me.

"What's wrong?" Miss Kate quickly asked.

She was sitting in her chair with Precious on her lap, sipping her coffee. Time had been rough on Miss Kate, and it showed in her body. Besides her unmistakable limp, she looked old.

Precious didn't look good either. Whatever was wrong with her was getting worse—much worse. I could see it on Miss Kate's face and on Precious.

She had lost a lot of weight in just the last week. I think Miss Kate knew that things were bad for her best friend. I watched as she rocked back and forth, cradling the cat. She was singing softly to her.

"Miss Kate, I want to give you something," I said.

She looked at me with a strange look. I went over and handed Miss Kate the envelope. She opened it and started counting all the money. Before she even finished, she looked up at me with an astonished look.

"What's this for?" she asked quietly.

"It's for you…well…it's more for Precious. There should be enough money to take her to the vet in Craig and get her fixed up," I said.

"Mom and Dad will be over in a minute. They're going to take Precious to Dr. Matthews in town," I said.

"Why can't I take her?" she questioned.

"Because we have something we need to do together," I answered.

-33-

"What do we need to do?" she quickly asked.

I looked at my watch; it was 4:00 p.m.

"We have eighteen hours before we need to be at Garner's Grocery Store," I said.

"Why would we go there? I don't want anything to do with those people," she answered quickly.

"That's when you're going to win the Elk Pole contest, claim the $250 gift card, and save me from Max Wilson," I said.

At first Miss Kate seemed shocked, but then a strange look went over her face.

"Did you say *Max Wilson?* Is that Principal Wilson's son?" she asked.

"Yeah, do you know them?" I asked.

"Of course, I know them. The Wilsons have been trying to get on my property for years to hunt. Two years ago, I caught him trespassing on the back side of the ranch, looking for elk."

"Is his son anything like him?" she asked.

"Much worse," I said. I told her about my first week at Pine Bluff, and she sat listening to the entire story.

"I hate this little town. Don't they have anything better to do than talk about everyone else?"

I stopped her. "Trust me, Miss Kate. Please don't judge the entire town on a couple of people. I made that mistake once, and I promised myself I won't make it again," I said.

I told her about Owen, Tommy, and Jesse, and how for the first time in my life I had friends—true friends. She sat listening to everything.

"I still don't see how I can help you," she said.

"We need to head up the mountain tonight and find Boss. You need to bring him in and win the

Elk Pole," I said. I could tell she finally understood my plan.

"That's impossible! I'm sorry, but I can't help you do that," she said and turned away.

-34-

Impossible? If I had learned anything this week, I had learned that nothing is impossible.

Just then I heard a car pull into the driveway. I walked over and carefully lifted Precious from Miss Kate's lap. She leaned over and gave the cat a kiss, passed me the envelope, and sighed in relief.

Dad was approaching the back door, and I headed out to meet him. I handed him the cat and the envelope.

"Dad, I'll see you tomorrow at Garner's. Make sure you're there at noon," I said.

Dad looked hesitant. "Hunter, are sure about this?" he asked.

"Dad, I've never been so sure about anything in my life. Just please stick to the plan," I said.

I went back into the living room and sat down.

"You know I've tried getting Boss for a number of years. He's a smart bull; everyone around town wants him," she said as she stared out the window.

Then she added as she pointed above her, "I even got his spot picked out." I looked up and saw the gap between the other elk and knew she had wanted to hang Boss there. He would be her greatest trophy.

"What's stopping you?" I asked.

Miss Kate took a deep breath and leaned back in her chair. She started slowly rocking.

"Each day I'm getting older, and I feel it. I'm no spring chicken, and my body reminds me every morning. I know where Boss lives; I've no doubt about that," she said.

"Then why, Miss Kate? What's stopping you?" I asked again.

"I can't make it up that side of the mountain, or I would've shot that giant years ago. I tried many times and failed. And it's just too hard for me now," she said.

"But in the past, you always went alone. You're not alone anymore, Miss Kate. I'm going to go with you. We're going to do it together," I said as I reached in the bag and pulled out my cowboy hat.

Miss Kate giggled.

"Where did you find that old thing?" she asked.

"Don't you worry, little lady. I'll ensure your safety up that mountain," I said in my best western voice.

Spending the night in the mountains would be new to me, but I felt it would be safe with Miss Kate. I was sure she would know exactly where to camp for the night and how to survive. She sent me out to the barn to grab the tent that hung on the south wall. After about thirty short minutes, we were packed and ready to go.

"I think we have everything we need for the night," she said.

She walked over and handed me one of the backpacks. It was heavy and filled with the basic necessities. Miss Kate always lived basic, so I wasn't counting on a four-star dinner that night.

Working on Miss Kate's ranch had changed me in more ways than one.

She grabbed her rifle and a box of shells.

"I think we have everything we need now," Miss Kate said as she threw me a flashlight.

"Yep, I think so," I said.

"There's one more thing," she said.

I quickly looked around. I thought we had everything packed and were prepared to head up the into the mountain.

Miss Kate turned and looked at me.

"Thanks, Hunter," she said in a low, sweet voice.

I did the only thing I could think of—I tipped my cowboy hat to her.

-35-

We climbed for a couple hours up the mountain. It had been dark for about an hour when we finally stopped.

"We're close. Let's make camp here," Miss Kate said.

I couldn't tell where we were, but she knew. I was amazed at how she moved up the mountain. Even at her age and with her limp, she moved better than I did. I had never even stepped foot on a mountainside until today.

Snow started to fall as we set up the tent. We were high enough up the mountain to see the lights of Pine Bluff. The forecast was calling for a couple inches of snow overnight, and I prayed we would get it. We already had a small base layer of snow on the ground around home, but we needed more for my plan to work.

It only took about twenty minutes for us to set up camp, and Miss Kate soon had a roaring fire going. She pulled out a couple pots and hung them over the fire. That night we ate canned venison and elk stew. I was starving, and it tasted amazing.

"What's the game plan for tomorrow?" I asked.

"You see that tiny light way over there?" she asked as she pointed to a faint glow of light. It had to be miles away.

"That's my ranch," she said. I looked farther north and could see another light and knew it was my house.

I turned and pointed between the two houses. "So Boss is somewhere around there," I said.

Miss Kate smiled. "Yep, he's right there in that valley," she said confidently. I could tell we had walked around the valley with the wind at our back the entire time. She had known that we couldn't take a chance of the herd's getting wind of us, or everything would be ruined.

"He usually travels with about eight to ten cows and a couple of smaller bulls," she said.

"How will I know it's him?" I asked.

Miss Kate smiled, "You won't have any doubt. He's the herd bull, and he's huge." She added, "The hard part will be getting down into the valley. That's why I've never been able to get Boss. It's steep, real steep."

"But you've never had help before," I reminded her quickly.

As we had gotten higher onto the mountain, I began to understand why Miss Kate hadn't tried to pursue Boss. The rocky, steep slopes made the trip almost impossible for someone alone. There were dangerous cliffs and rocky edges in all directions. This was definitely a two-person job. And up until now, Miss Kate had always been alone.

And so have I.

-36-

It was surprisingly warm when I crawled into the sleeping bag Miss Kate had packed for me. Even though it was cold and snow was coming down, I had no problem falling asleep. I didn't know if it was from the tiring walk up the mountain or that I was finally at peace.

Every once in a while, I would wake up because Miss Kate would leave the tent to add wood to the fire. But for the most part, it was the best sleep I had ever had.

I woke up to the smell of bacon cooking on the fire. It was still dark, and Miss Kate was preparing breakfast for both of us. The stars still filled the sky, reminding me of the view of the city landscape in Denver.

But out here, there was no noise. No one was pushing or shoving their way to get on a bus or honking their car horns impatiently. It was just the two of us and nature.

"We need to eat fast. We should be near the bottom of the valley at first light. It's our only chance to catch Boss sneaking through," Miss Kate said.

I ate fast, but she had already packed the tent by the time I finished my last bite of eggs. We threw our packs over our backs and headed down the mountain toward the nearby valley.

At first the hiking was easy, but it soon became steep and more dangerous with every step. There were two spots where we had to use a rope and help each other down. I knew there was no way Miss Kate or anyone else could have made the trip by themselves.

After a good hour, the mountains finally started to level out into the valley. I was thankful when my feet felt level ground. I said a little prayer and looked toward the sky. The stars were gone, and the sun was just starting to come up.

Miss Kate pointed toward a thick bunch of pines on the edge of the valley and motioned for me to follow her. It was about a quarter mile walk, and she was moving at such a fast pace I almost had to jog.

After a couple minutes, we reached the pines. Miss Kate looked around and pointed toward some fallen trees near the edge of the woods. We went over and tucked ourselves among the trees. Everything was covered in snow from the previous night. It was a perfect spot that would provide good cover for us to ambush Boss. She got her rifle ready and set it on a branch.

"Now what?" I asked. For some reason, I thought we would sit down, and the elk would walk in front of us, and it would be over. Having never hunted, I had no idea what to expect.

"Now we wait," she said.

I looked at my watch. We didn't have much time to wait. We had to be at Garner's at noon or else I was a dead man. I knew that for sure.

"Don't worry; it will happen," said Miss Kate.

I trusted her. I sat back and watched the valley come to life as the sun rose over the horizon. The first animal we saw was a small mule deer buck. He looked like he had two points on each side. He moved in front of us about a hundred yards away, milling through the valley.

"He's lucky I'm not hungry," Miss Kate said with a smile.

About twenty minutes went by, and I began to get nervous. We were starting to run out of time.

Without warning, Miss Kate reached over and tapped my leg. I looked up and saw a huge brown object moving through the woods in front of us. The elk was easy to spot in the snow-covered woods. It came out into the valley a couple of hundred yards away. It didn't have any horns, but it was a good sign that we were in the right spot.

A couple of minutes later, I saw more elk moving through the valley. What an amazing sight! The elk looked huge as they moved gracefully through the snow.

———

Suddenly the entire herd stopped and turned to look behind them. Within seconds, we heard a loud, echoing bugle shake the trees. There was no doubt—it was Boss!

-37-

The huge bull elk finally showed himself.

Miss Kate was right—there was no doubt who was in charge on this mountain. I didn't need to ask; I knew that was our bull. His rack was massive! It made all the other elk—even the ones mounted in Miss Kate's house—look small.

The other elk continued to feed into the valley, coming out right in front of us. The wind was still in our face, and everything was going as Miss Kate and I had planned.

Boss was in no hurry as he meandered toward the other elk feeding in the valley. He was just about to enter the field when the other elk stopped and looked directly toward us. At that exact same moment, the wind shifted; I felt it against my back.

"Oh, no, a mountain thermal! The wind has changed," Miss Kate whispered.

It was now or never. The cows picked up their tails and started to jog off back into the deep timber. Boss stood alarmed, watching as the entire herd entered the woods and passed him.

He stood watching, protecting the other elk. But he had stayed too long.

BOOM! The sound of the rifle in the cold pine forest spooked me as much as the surrounding valley. Snow fell off above us, covering both of us. I jumped up and wiped the snow off my face to look.

All of the elk were gone. There was no sign of any of them. I turned and looked at Miss Kate.

"Did you hit him?" I asked.

"I'm not sure. I had to hurry the shot and didn't have a good rest," she said disappointed.

I crawled out of our hiding spot and started to walk in the general direction of the last place I'd seen Boss.

The snow was much deeper in the valley and made it hard to walk. It took me a couple of minutes, but I finally made it over near the spot where the elk had been. I looked around in the woods and couldn't see anything but white. Miss Kate was right behind me, scanning the ground.

"Look for blood," she said.

I started walking around, looking for any sign of a hit. I could see the tracks of the elk that made it look like a couple trucks had gone through the woods, but there was no mistaking the elk tracks in the snow.

Miss Kate walked up. "Any luck?" she asked.

"Nothing," I said shaking my head sadly.

She turned and looked back toward the pine timber where we had sat, studying the angle. "He was farther that way," she finally said as she pointed toward the north. I continued that way, scanning the ground for any sign.

After a couple of feet, I ran into trackless snow. "Keep going closer to those trees," she said, pointing off to the right.

After a little while, I found some tracks again. This time it was only one set of tracks, and they were really big.

I started to follow them, and after about twenty yards, I saw something. I bent down, and sure enough it was blood. She had hit Boss!

"Miss Kate, I found something!" I yelled.

She hobbled toward me as fast as she could, and we stared at a couple drops of blood in the snow. We followed the tracks for another couple of minutes, finding blood drops along the way.

"Hunter!" Miss Kate gasped.

I looked up and saw Boss!

-38-

The huge elk was lying dead against two trees. His head was leaning against the second tree, pushing his massive antlers high into the sky.

Miss Kate and I hugged. We ran up to the bull, and I held his massive horns. She knelt down and looked like she was praying.

"It's 10:00 a.m., and we're deep in the valley, Hunter. I don't see how there's any chance we can make it to town by noon."

"Don't worry, pretty lady, I have a plan," I said in my cowboy voice.

I reached in my pocket and pulled out a cell phone. I turned it on, but it just beeped.

"No signal!" I said in disbelief.

"There's no way you can use that thing here in the valley. We're blocked on both sides by the mountains," she said.

I didn't have long to think. I had to make a decision.

"I'm going to run back up the mountain until I get a signal," I told Miss Kate.

"Are you sure? That could be dangerous," she warned me.

"I got this. It's our only hope of making it on time. We've come too far to give up now," I said. "By the way, what's the name of this valley?"

"Tell them we're at Primal Point between Stag Mountain and Riggen's Valley," Miss Kate said.

Perfect. I took off running, following our original tracks. I cleared the pine timber and quickly found myself heading back up the mountain. Every little bit I'd stop and check for a signal. I finally found it just ten minutes up the mountain. I could barely see Miss Kate down in the valley.

My hands were cold and wet from walking up

the mountain. I fumbled to punch in the number and finally got it. The voice on the other end was music to my ears.

"Hello."

"Owen, it's Hunter," I said and gave him the directions Miss Kate had told me.

I went back down the mountain and joined her. By this time, she already had the elk gutted.

"They're on their way," I said.

"Who? I didn't think anyone would ever want to help me," said Miss Kate.

"Well, you're wrong," I said and smiled.

We both sat admiring the giant elk. I was hooked. There was no doubt that I'd be an elk hunter for the rest of my life. We sat talking and laughing for about twenty minutes until we heard the distant sound of snowmobiles. The sound got louder and louder, and within minutes three snowmobiles pulled up.

"Miss Kate, I'd like to introduce you to my three best friends—Owen, Jesse, and Tommy."

The three boys jumped off their sleds to greet

Miss Kate. She didn't know what to say. She was still having trouble believing that they were there to help her.

"Where's Boss? We don't have much time," Owen said.

I pointed behind us, and all three of the boys stood in amazement.

"Wow, that's the biggest elk I've ever seen!" Tommy exclaimed.

"How many points is it?" Jesse asked.

"It's an 8 x 8," Miss Kate said and smiled.

"We'll have time to admire it when it's hanging on the Elk Pole at Garner's. Let's hook it up to the snowmobiles and get to town!" I said.

The boys grabbed two big, tow ropes and hooked Boss up behind the snowmobiles. The fresh snow was just enough to carry the huge beast down the valley and toward town. It didn't take us long to get down the mountain on the sleds.

I looked at my watch, and it read 11:50 a.m. We only had ten minutes to make it to town!

-39-

We hit the field between Miss Kate's ranch and our house with Boss behind us. There were little tracks on Redemption Road as we blasted toward town. During the ride there, I couldn't help but think that some divine intervention was involved. So many things could have gone wrong with our plan but hadn't.

The sleds pulled into town, and we could see a huge crowd gathering at Garner's. The adults were there to see the winner of the annual Elk Pole, and all the kids were there to see the big fight.

The entire town of Pine Bluff was awaiting our arrival. We pulled in like rock stars. Everyone cheered and pointed as Boss was dragged in. Almost everyone cheered.

"They're too late; it's already 12:01 p.m." yelled a man from the back. The crowd turned and saw it was Mr. Wilson.

"Technically, the rules say they need to be here by 12:00 p.m. They were in the parking lot on time," said a different voice. He added, "I'd like to be the first to congratulate Hunter and his friends. They are this year's winner of our annual Elk Pole contest!"

"That's my dad," Owen whispered.

The crowd cheered.

Miss Kate stepped off the back of Jesse's snowmobile and took off her helmet. The cheers instantly stopped, and everyone stared, wondering why she was there.

I walked slowly up to the stage and grabbed the mic. As I motioned for Miss Kate to join me on stage, I could see people whispering and pointing. The happy scene had changed; suddenly people were frowning.

I stood on the stage as Miss Kate hesitantly

walked up to join me. "I didn't shoot Boss; Miss Kate did," I announced. I heard a bunch of gasps and more whispering. Out of the corner of my eye, I saw Max. He was surrounded by a bunch of his friends and his dad. He didn't look happy, and neither did Mr. Wilson. Miss Kate's elk had knocked him out of the lead and put him in second place.

I moved the podium out of the way and stood proudly next to Miss Kate. I felt so bad for her, and I could tell she just wanted to get out of Pine Bluff and back to the safety of her ranch.

I turned and motioned to my dad who was standing over by our car. He opened the trunk and grabbed a bucket. He slowly walked in front of the crowd and tipped the bucket over.

Stones went everywhere; there had to be at least 300 of them. He bent down and picked up two of them. He walked over and handed one to Mr. Wilson and one to Max. The entire crowd was silent. They were looking at Mr. Wilson and the stones on the ground.

"Who's first?" I asked into the mic.

Whispers started to circulate among the people as they stared at the pile of stones.

"Who's first?" I asked again.

I added, "Who's the one that wants to cast the first stone?" I asked.

I stood on the stage next to Kate. People were looking around at each other and then at the stage.

Suddenly my parents and Owen, Jesse, and Tommy joined us on stage.

The crowd stood silent, waiting for someone to say something.

I finally spoke.

"I've learned a lot since moving to Pine Bluff. I finally have real friends. I haven't played video games in over a week, but most of all, I've learned to love my neighbor. And in a town as small as Pine Bluff, aren't we all neighbors?" I asked.

The entire parking lot was silent. I could tell by the look on everyone's face that they finally understood.

Slowly the crowd started to surge forward with smiles on their faces. Out of the corner of my eye,

I saw Miss Kate. She looked great! Her face had a certain glow—like years of pain had been washed away. She was soon surrounded by townspeople hugging her. I could tell they were sorry for the way they had treated her.

As I stood there admiring the emotional scene, I felt a big, cold hand on my shoulder.

I turned to see Max. He looked different too.

"Hey kid, what's your name?" he asked me.

"Hunter," I said.

Max chuckled loudly and stuck out his hand. "Welcome to Pine Bluff, Hunter," he said.

No more City Boy. It was right there at Garner's Grocery Store where a town healed, and lives were changed—all because of one video game-addicted city boy; one crazy, widowed rancher; and an elk named Boss.

No stones were thrown that day or any day afterward. That day went down in Pine Bluff history as a day when the townspeople celebrated the hunting skills of a woman they now called *Miss Kate.*

About the Author

Lane Walker is an award-winning author, speaker, and educator. His book collection, Hometown Hunters, won a Bronze Medal at the Moonbeam Awards for Best Kids series.

Lane is an accomplished outdoor writer in Michigan. He has been writing for the past 15 years and has over 250 articles professionally published. Walker has a real passion for hunter recruitment and getting kids in the outdoors. He is a former teacher and current principal living in Michigan with his wife and four kids.

Lane is a highly sought-after professional speaker traveling to schools, churches and wild game dinners.

To book Lane for an event or to find out more check out www.lanewalkerbooks.com or contact him at info@lanewalkerbooks.com.